诗词遇见
杭州

Hangzhou
Through Poetry

（中英文）

云春　亚玲　编著
［美］亦歌　译

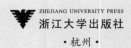

ZHEJIANG UNIVERSITY PRESS
浙江大学出版社
·杭州·

图书在版编目(CIP)数据

诗词遇见杭州：汉英对照 / 云春，亚玲编著 ；
(美)亦歌译. — 杭州：浙江大学出版社，2023.3(2023.8 重印)
ISBN 978-7-308-23184-8

Ⅰ．①诗… Ⅱ．①云… ②亚… ③亦… Ⅲ．①古典诗
歌—诗集—中国—汉、英 Ⅳ．①I222

中国版本图书馆 CIP 数据核字(2022)第 193837 号

诗词遇见杭州(中英文)

云　春　亚　玲　编著
[美]亦　歌　译

策划编辑	吴伟伟
责任编辑	宁　檬　曲　静
责任校对	陈逸行
封面设计	周　灵
出版发行	浙江大学出版社
	(杭州市天目山路 148 号　邮政编码 310007)
	(网址：http://www.zjupress.com)
排　　版	杭州朝曦图文设计有限公司
印　　刷	浙江省邮电印刷股份有限公司
开　　本	880mm×1230mm　1/32
印　　张	10.75
字　　数	190 千
版 印 次	2023 年 3 月第 1 版　2023 年 8 月第 2 次印刷
书　　号	ISBN 978-7-308-23184-8
定　　价	68.00 元

●●● 前　言 ●●●

　　被马可·波罗誉为"世界上最美丽华贵之城"的杭州，理应被更多国内外读者所知晓。 在国际交流日益深入、对外话语体系迅速完善的全球化语境中，讲故事是国际传播的最佳方式。在杭州 2022 年亚运盛会举办前夕，《诗词遇见杭州（中英文）》的付梓恰逢其时。 杭州是中国七大古都之一，有 3000 多年的悠久历史，其素以美丽山水著称于世，古今文人吟咏赞赏从未断绝。 杭州也是一片佛教圣地，每年春季，六桥三竺，佛徒香客摩肩接踵；灵隐古刹，佛事兴盛，湖光山色又多了几分神秘灵韵。 中国民间 "上有天堂，下有苏杭" 的两句俚语，便是对其城市风貌最好的概括。 今天的杭州既是繁华的文明都市，又是岁时轮回的自然情人。 以西湖、大运河、钱塘江文化为代表的杭州，在开放中融合，在创新中发展，于全球发展格局中大大地提升了国际影响力。 西湖文化融山水园林、历史文化、宗教民俗于一体；运河文化集水利商贸、物产水景于一身。 "钱塘郭里看潮人，直至白头看不足。"滚滚钱塘潮涌，依旧群龙，涛卷霜雪，壮观天下无。

　　以诗词描绘杭州的历史文化空间，是一个极具人文情怀的举措。 杭州历史上曾经历了无数盛衰变易，沉浮更迭。 春秋时期杭州归属越国，战国时并入楚国。 秦国统一中国，置钱唐县。 隋代钱唐扩大，成为杭州府治。 唐朝一统天下，为避国号，始称钱塘。 五代十国，钱镠治国有方，外御强敌，内修政治，吴越都城（今杭州）遂成东南名都。 宋朝建国，杭州风景已经十分可观。 然宋室南渡，偏安杭州，更名临安。 南宋苟且偷安，轻社稷，终致悲剧。 杭州古称武林、钱塘，素以山水形势见胜，引无数文人雅士歌咏流连；古都杭州见证了多少朝代的起落沉浮，激起仁人志士的扼腕悲叹。

　　关于杭州的诗词，经年累月积淀下来已十分浩繁。 《诗词遇见杭州（中英文）》最终斟酌勘定百首，实属不易。 在数字人文时代，对数量可观的作品进行披沙拣金倒也不是太难之事。编选真正的困难之处在于，优中择优，精选百首。 此书篇目几易其稿，最终经过编者和译者的多次辨析商榷，依据并兼顾两个原则，选定百首。 这里的诗词不限于历时性意义上的古代诗歌，而是包括了广义文体意义上的古诗，因此也有少量的近现代名家如苏曼殊、毛泽东等人的作品选列其中。 所选诗词主要参考了以下文献：上海辞书出版社的《唐诗鉴赏辞典》（2017）、《宋诗鉴赏辞典》（2015）、《元明清诗鉴赏辞典》（2018）、《元明清词鉴赏辞典》（2017），北京燕山出版社的《宋词鉴赏辞典》

(1987)等。"古诗文网"也为编写带来了许多方便，在此谨致谢忱。

《说文解字》之中的"百"，意为"十十也"，本义是计数数字，但也有完美圆满之意。这本书的两条编选原则是：（1）仅选取名家代表作之一二。白居易与苏轼都曾任职杭州，写下了不少名篇，但也仅选其二三代表作品，这样才能在有限的篇幅里包罗更多的作者，立体地进入杭州的历史文化空间。例如，苏轼写钱塘观潮的好诗不少，也有在杭州吉祥寺为牡丹与陈襄"斗诗"的作品，但都让位于《饮湖上初晴后雨》。这样的编选原则虽有挂一漏万的遗憾，但百首最终包揽了82位诗人。一些算不上传统意义上的大家名家的优秀作品也被挑选列入，以飨读者。如唐代诗人牟融、李廓、长孙佐辅，宋代词人高观国、李新、谢翱，明代诗人张煌言等。（2）主题广泛。所选诗词主题包括杭州的山水自然、宗教人文、民俗风物等方方面面。西湖美景、钱塘潮涌是诗词歌咏的主角，但编选的时候也特别纳入了宫室寺庙、名山古刹、美食民俗等主题，以便让读者探索中国传统人文幽微的精神空间。清代姚思勤的《东郊土物藕粉》入选，就是其中一例。仲殊的《诉衷情·寒食》写寒食节西湖独特的热闹盛景，可圈可点。杭州晴日柔暖，西湖雾气微蒙，山麓画楼，佳丽欢笑。词人从"三千"写到"一片云头"，有一种繁华散尽、身如浮云的生命参悟。表面上是写民俗节日，实则是文人雅士精神世界的敞亮。 再如宋仁宗《赐梅挚知杭州》一诗，记录了古代君臣间交往的儒雅风流，也传递了一段文坛佳话。 梅挚根据宋仁宗的"地有湖山美"在杭州修建了一座有美堂，以示感谢上恩。 1059 年，欧阳修作有经典散文《有美堂记》，纪念这段人情故事。 今天，有美堂已无影无踪，但诗词中的人事之美，可烛照当今读者内心的人文渴求。

城市空间与山水自然是人类情感意识的居所。 诗词里的西湖十里荷花、断桥残雪、南屏晚钟、九里云松等意象早在读者心里定格为艺术画面。 中国诗词历来重隐秀之美，多有文外之重旨。 诗词或感遇感怀，或咏怀咏史，或观览盛景，直抒胸臆。诗词的鉴赏历来难以满足读者的多方期待。 本书的中文鉴赏部分既重发掘诗歌的情怀也重语言艺术。 诗词若有用事用典之处，则参考史料、文献阐明语境，说事论典，有助于读者进入诗歌的情境与意境，引领读者深入作品更丰富细腻的情韵层面。若是观览盛景直抒胸臆的诗词，中文鉴赏部分则强调其语言修辞和独特兴发的美感，点明其所铺陈、所比兴的对象。 如《杭州故人信至齐安》一诗的中文鉴赏部分既指出了苏轼与杭州故友的真挚友情，又介绍了杭州美食自晒荔干、红螺酱和西庵茶等。

《诗词遇见杭州（中英文）》中文鉴赏部分的原则是：百字美文，破除窠臼，精准典雅，浮言勿用。 全书中文鉴赏部分单篇不超过两百字。

译事之难，人人皆知。中国诗词的外译更是需要"知其不可为而为之"的勇气、胆识与敬畏之心。严复先生在《天演论》中的"译例言"中讲道："译事三难：信、达、雅。求其信，已大难矣！顾信矣，不达，虽译，犹不译也，则达尚焉。"译者亦歌为杭州人，毕业于浙江师范大学英语系，熟稔中西文学，有长达数十年的在美国从教经历。他采用地道典雅的当代英文，遵循意为先、音形次之的原则，力求忠实于原文，避免因强求押韵而损害原意，努力使中国诗词之美能跨越语言和文化的藩篱，引起国外读者的共鸣。

本书旨在献礼杭州 2022 年亚运会，共襄华夏人文盛事。以白居易、林逋、苏轼、弘历、袁枚等 82 位诗人优雅的声音叙述杭州故事，还原他们与杭州山水的深挚情缘。杭州乃山水之城、人文之城，百首精选诗词为城市地理人文典范塑形，挖掘现代都市的诗学空间与美学价值。中英双语鉴赏翻译，用英语讲好中国故事，提升中文读者全球胜任力，提升城市的国际形象。

本书在策划、编写与出版过程中，得到了中外语言合作交流中心、杭州市西湖区有关部门、浙江大学出版社、成都大学海外教育学院及其他众多人士的鼎力相助。本书的中文鉴赏部分主要由四川外国语大学刘云春教授，美国新罕布什尔大学孔子学院原中方院长、成都大学斯特灵学院副教授刘亚玲，以及美国新罕布什尔大学孔子学院原外方院长、成都大学外国语学院和海外教育学院特聘研究员王亦歌共同完成；英文翻译工作全部由王亦歌承担；英文编辑和校对工作由美国新罕布什尔大学英文系教授、博士生导师莫妮卡·邱，以及英国伦敦国王学院的艾莉·洛克女士完成。莫妮卡和艾莉女士对诗词译文及注释提出了大量宝贵意见，使本书得以按时完稿，对此深表谢意！

● ● ◉ Preface ◉ ● ●

Described by Marco Polo as the most magnificent and luxurious metropolis of the world, Hangzhou should be known to more readers. As global exchanges and frameworks for international discourse improve and expand around the world, storytelling is the best international media. The publication of *Hangzhou Through Poetry* is timely before the grand opening of Asian Games Hangzhou 2022. As one of the seven ancient capitals of China, Hangzhou boasts more than 3000 years of long history and unrivaled natural scenery. Since ancient times, Chinese literati have never stopped praising and appreciating its beauty. Hangzhou is also known as a sacred land of Buddhism. Every spring, pilgrims crowd shoulder to shoulder upon its arched bridges and in Buddhist temples. The spectacular Buddhist ceremonies at the ancient Lingyin Temple are famons, and attach a spiritual charm to the mountains and lakes of Hangzhou. The saying in China, "Paradise in heaven, Suzhou and Hangzhou on Earth, " best sums up the city's features. Hangzhou today is not only a bustling, culturally advanced metropolis, but also a gem of natural beauty amidst city life. Characterized by rich culture mixed with the scenery of the West Lake, the Grand Canal and the Qiantang River, Hangzhou integrates and develops through openness and innovation, which enhances its international influence within the framework of global development. The culture of the West Lake materializes through its mountains, waters and gardens, history as well as religion and folk customs; and the culture of the Grand Canal incorporates its irrigation engineering, facilitation of trade transportation, produce and waterscape as well.

"Admiring the tidal bore surfers outside the City of Qiantang, they never cease to amaze you! " The mighty tidal bores of Qiantang rage on, as their huge waves roll up mountainous foams of frost and snow, impressive and unseen elsewhere in the world.

It is such a humanistic endeavor to access the historical and cultural heritage of Hangzhou through classic poems. Hangzhou has witnessed many cyclical booms and busts, rises and declines. The city was under the rule of the Kingdom of Yue during the

Spring and Autumn period but relegated to Chu during the Warring States period. Qiantang was established as a county after Qin reunited China. After expansion in the Sui Dynasty, Hangzhou became a prefecture. To avoid using the same name of the Tang Dynasty, Qiantang changed its "tang" to a different character. During the Five Dynasties and Ten Kingdoms period, Qian Liu ruled the kingdom effectively by defending against powerful enemies and encouraging upright politics, thus turning this capital city of Wu-Yue into a festive metropolis of the southeast. After the establishment of the Song Dynasty, the scenery of Hangzhou was already very impressive. Later, the Song Dynasty court sought refuge south of the Yangtze River and settled in Hangzhou, content with partial sovereignty. The Southern Song Dynasty took comfort in the temporary and tentative peace, but neglected the welfare of the state, which eventually led to tragedy. Endowed with splendid natural beauty, Hangzhou was known as Wulin, Qiantang, and other names in ancient times and was subject of many writings and sought-after place for the literati. The ancient capital of Hangzhou has witnessed numerous dynasties' rises and declines, as well as laments and sighs of the righteous and noble-minded.

A voluminous collection of classic poems and lyrics about Hangzhou has developed over the years. It was no easy task to select 100 candidate poems. In the era of digital humanities, it is no challenge to peruse through archives for 100 good ones; the real challenge is to pick out the best of the best. The process was challenging and meticulous, and many a time we had to part reluctantly with our treasured poems. The content of this book has seen many changes and replacements. After many debates and exchanges among the editors and the translator, 100 of the most beautiful poems of Hangzhou were finally selected following two rules. The poems selected are not strictly ancient in their historical context, but with flexible content, therefore, readers will find such modern or contemporary poets such as Su Manshu and Mao Zedong. The main reference books for poem selection include the *Dictionary of the Tang Dynasty Poetry Appreciation* (2017), *Dictionary of the Song Dynasty Poetry Appreciation* (2015), *Dictionary of the Yuan, Ming & Qing Dynasty Poetry Appreciation* (2018), *Dictionary of the Yuan, Ming & Qing Dynasty Lyrics Appreciation* (2017), and *Dictionary of Song Dynasty Lyrics Appreciation* (1987). Online Classic

Poems' resources were also a great help. We express our heartfelt thanks here! According to *Shuowen Jiezi*, "one hundred" means ten times ten. Though used as a numerical, it nevertheless contains the connotation of "complete" or "perfect". The two rules for poem selection were: (1) Only two to three per master poet were chosen as representative works. Both Bai Juyi and Su Shi had tenures in Hangzhou and left numerous masterpieces, yet we had to limit the selections to two or three pieces to include a greater range of poets, to chronologically portray the historical and cultural space of Hangzhou within limited space. For instance, Su Shi penned many excellent poems about tidal bore viewing, as well as competing poems about moutans in Auspicious Temple with Chen Xiang, but we selected his "Drinking on the Lake with Drizzles after a Short Clearance" instead. Although such selection may inevitably mean that for one selected, ten thousand others are left out, this book is able to include the works of 82 great poets. The works of some lesser-known poets were also included for the readers such as Mou Rong, Li Kuo, Zhangsun Zuofu of the Tang Dynasty, Gao Guanguo, Li Xin and Xie Ao of the Song Dynasty, and Zhang Huangyan of the Ming Dynasty. (2) The collection should include a wide range of topics. The selected poems range from nature to religious humanism, folk customs, and other topics. Though West Lake scenery and the Qiantang tidal bore are two main categories, there are also poems on palaces, temples, famous mountains and monasteries, culinary arts and folk traditions. They enable readers to step into the Chinese traditional humanities' subtle spiritual space. The selection of Qing Dynasty poet Yao Siqin's "A Lake East Delicacy: Lotus Root Starch" is one such case. Zhongshu's "To the Tune of Pouring Out Your Heart—The Cold Food Festival" is about the remarkable festive scene of West Lake during the Cold Food Festival. Hangzhou's sunny days are mild, as mists and fog partially conceal the lake, with painted mansions dotting foothills and beauties enjoying leisure with hearty laughter. The lyrics begin with "three thousand" and end with "one drifting cloud", offering a life insight that after all splendor fades into ash, only drifting clouds dot the sky. Though it is about folk culture, it nevertheless illuminates for us the inner world of the Chinese literati. Another example is Renzong, the Emperor of Song's poem "Granting Mei Zhi Governorship of Hangzhou," which not only generated a wonderful literary anecdote, but also illustrated the admirable cultured and refined relationships between the emperor and their court officials of ancient China. Following Renzong's line, "known for its beautiful mountains and lake, " Mei Zhi constructed the Hall of Youmei to express his gratitude for the emperor's trust. In 1059, Ouyang Xiu wrote a classic piece of prose, *An Account of the Hall of Youmei*, to commemorate this tale of trust and favor. Although the Hall of Youmei mentioned in the poems is long gone, such wonderful interactions in the past nevertheless cast light upon the humanistic quest within every contemporary reader's heart.

Urban spaces and natural landscapes are dwellings of emotional consciousness for humans. The imageries of West Lake's ten li of lotus blossoms, and famous scenes of Remnant Snow on Bridge Duan, Evening Bell Tolls at Nanping, Nine li of Cloudy Pines in classic poetry have long been framed as artistic pictures in readers' minds. Classic Chinese poetry is known for carrying implicit connotations with hidden feelings and ambitions beyond surface words. Therefore, classic poetry can be used to express gratitude for help or encouragement received, emotional recollections, expressing one's feelings, commenting on history, feasting on beautiful sceneries, or laying bare one's mind. Poetry digests face challenges in meeting various expectations from readers. The Chinese digests of this book focus on uncovering the poems sentiments and feelings as well as the art of word choices. For poems with allusions, we refer to historical records to expound on their contexts to help readers grasp the poems' artistic conceptions and situations, to guide readers to approach the rich and exquisite artistic charm of the works. For poems on scenery or expressing one's mind, the Chinese digests lay emphasis on their rhetoric and unique aesthetic feelings on their uplifting associations to cast light on what they are trying to elaborate on or compare. For example, "On Receiving a Letter in Qi'an from a Hangzhou Friend" not only reveals the sincere friendship between Su Shi and his friend, but also introduces tidbits of Hangzhou such as home-dried lichees, red snail sauce and tea from the West Monastery etc. Therefore, the rules of thumb for the Chinese digests were that they were to be written in short but elegant prose, avoid set patterns, and be accurate and refined without baseless comments. The digests of this book are all under two hundred characters.

Anyone knows translation is a daunting task. One needs to have insight and reverence in addition to the courage of "knowing that it cannot be done perfectly but to face the challenge head-on anyway" when translating classic Chinese poetry. Just as Mr. Yan Fu wrote in his "Introductory Remarks of Translation" of *Evolution and Ethics*: "Three things are the most challenging in translation: faithfulness, expressiveness and elegance. Trying to be faithful to the original is formidable enough! Pivoting towards "faithfulness", "expressiveness" suffers, and such translation is as good as no translation, therefore, "expressiveness" should be observed by all means." The translator of this book is Yige, a native of Hangzhou, who graduated from the English Department of Zhejiang Normal University. He is familiar with topics of Chinese and English literature with decades of teaching experience in US. He tried to use authentic and elegant contemporary English in translation. Following the rule of content and imagery first, music and metric pattern second, the translations are meant to be faithful to the originals instead of following the original rhyming scheme and pattern so as not to alter the original meaning. We hope such artistic translations of classic Chinese poetry can cross language and cultural boundaries and resonate with contemporary readers outside China.

It is our hope to contribute to the grand opening of the Asian Games Hangzhou 2022, and to participate in this magnificent humanistic undertaking as well. Through the graceful voices of 82 poets including Bai Juyi, Lin Bu, Su Shi, Hongli, Yuan Mei, narrative stories about Hangzhou unfold. The poets' earnest affections for the mountains and waters of Hangzhou are revived. Hangzhou is a scenic city, as well as a city of humanities. The selected 100 poems shape the city's human geography and expand the city's poetics of space and aesthetic value. This Chinese and English translation work hopes to tell China's past stories and illuminate this international metropolis.

During planning, writing, and publishing stages for this book, we received sincere help and assistance from Center for Language Education and Cooperation, several Hangzhou Xihu District departments, Hangzhou Xihu District United Front Work Department, Returned Overseas Chinese Federation of Hangzhou Xihu District, Zhejiang University Press, Overseas Education College of Chengdu University, and many others.

The Chinese digests in this book are the works of Professor Yunchun Liu of Sichuan International Studies University, former Chinese Director of the Confucius Institute at University of New Hampshire, Associate Professor Yaling Liu of Chengdu University, and the former Director of the Confucius Institute at University of New Hampshire, Research Fellow of College of Foreign Languages and Cultures, Overseas Education College of Chengdu University, Yige Wang. English translation is the work of Yige Wang. The English editor and co-editor are University of New Hampshire English Professor, Monica Chiu, and Ellie Locke of King's College London. Our heartfelt thanks to Monica and Ellie who contributed greatly to the translations and English notes. This book would not be possible without their help.

目　录

CONTENTS

9

1. 小池

〔南宋〕杨万里

泉眼无声惜细流，树阴照水爱晴柔。

小荷才露尖尖角，早有蜻蜓立上头。

◆
◆
◆
◆

赏：杨万里的诗以活法新意著称，其七言绝句尤以妙趣横生、清新活泼自成风格，即"诚斋体"。诗中有泉眼、细流、树阴、晴柔、蜻蜓、小荷动静相宜，无声胜有声，流溢无限生机。此诗创作地点不详，但多认为是写杭州的荷花。

1. Little Pond

By Yang Wanli（1127－1206 Southern Song Dynasty）

The silent spring cherishes its trickling flow;

Reflected trees on the pond savor the sun's mild glow.

A tender lotus leaf just sprouted;

A dragonfly already perches on its tip.

◆
◆
◆
◆

Note：Yang Wanli wrote many poems about lotus blossoms in the West Lake. Many photographers are inspired by the theme to capture dragonflies on early blooming lotus leaves in the West Lake.

2. 宿杭州虚白堂

〔唐〕李郢

秋月斜明虚白堂，寒蛩唧唧树苍苍。

江风彻晓不得睡，二十五声秋点长。

◆
◆
◆
◆

赏：晚唐诗人李郢善写景状物，诗风老练沉郁。虚白堂位于杭州府城内旧治，堂内大石刻有白居易诗。"虚室生白"源自《庄子·人间世》，谓心中纯净无欲。诗人于虚白堂一夜所见所闻，无非秋月寒虫，江风彻夜不息，并无主观感叹。该诗以有声之物写出无声之境，以物观物，物我一体，颇有履德养空、恬神虚白的道家妙悟。

2. Lodging at the Xubai Hall of Hangzhou

By Li Ying (618—907 Tang Dynasty)

Autumn moonlight slants into the Xubai Hall;

Fall crickets chirp under verdant trees.

Chilly river breezes keep me awake

With autumn night's twenty-five beats clear and long.

❖
❖
❖
❖

Note: In ancient China, a night is divided into five watches with five counts per watch. Twenty-five beats make one night.

3. 青玉案·元夕

〔南宋〕辛弃疾

　　东风夜放花千树。 更吹落，星如雨。 宝马雕车香满路。凤箫声动，玉壶光转，一夜鱼龙舞。

　　蛾儿雪柳黄金缕。 笑语盈盈暗香去。 众里寻他千百度。蓦然回首，那人却在，灯火阑珊处。

◆
◆
◆
◆

　　赏:这是豪放词派领袖辛弃疾为数不多的婉约作品之一。南宋杭州元夕夜烟火盛况,赏灯裙屐欢声不断。然火树银花的热闹反衬着一个孤高寂寞、寻寻觅觅的人物形象。词人辛弃疾不被偏安王朝重用,政治失意多年,其作多寄托自己的感慨。梁启超先生称此词"自怜幽独,伤心人别有怀抱"。

3. To the Tune of Green Jade Plate—The Lantern Festival

By Xin Qiji (1140—1207 Southern Song Dynasty)

An easterly evening breeze sets a thousand trees abloom

As if dislodged stars

Shower the sky.

Ornate horse carriages leave a trail of fragrance.

Flutes and pipes sound，

The moon tilts，

Fish dragon parades march through the night.

Hair ornaments of paper butterflies and fantasias dazzle.

A faint aroma lingers after happy chatter.

I seek her in vain among the crowds

Turning around；

There she is！

Under lights dim and sparse.

◆

◆

◆

◆

Note: Renowned lyricist Xin Qiji wrote this famous lyric about Hangzhou's Lantern Festival accompanied by spectacular fireworks, as if "trees abloom and stars showering." This lyric is melancholy in tone, in that the bustling crowds intensify the poet's feelings of loneliness with no one in sight to talk to. This was written at a time when the Southern Song Dynasty faced imminent threat from the north. The poet's calls for war preparations fell on deaf ears.

4．卜算子·咏梅

〔南宋〕陆游

驿外断桥边，寂寞开无主。已是黄昏独自愁，更著风和雨。

无意苦争春，一任群芳妒。零落成泥碾作尘，只有香如故。

◆
◆
◆
◆

赏：自古文人多咏梅寄怀，但唐宋文人与六朝不同。虽都是宋人，陆游与林和靖也略有不同。林处士的暗香疏影重高人隐士的避世情怀，陆游"不争春、香如故"的梅花意象则为失意志士孤高兀傲的形象。虽此词创作地点不详，断桥也并非一定是西湖的断桥，但很多人认为此词与西湖边的梅花有关。

4. To the Tune of Divination Ditty—Ode to Plum Blossoms

By Lu You (1125－1210 Southern Song Dynasty)

Outside the lodging post by the broken bridge

A plum blossom blooms unvisited.

Alone and melancholy at evenfall

Further battered by wind and rain.

Vying not for spring's attention

Nonchalant to the jealousy of other flowers.

Even when unpetaled, trampled to dust

Its fragrance lingers.

◆
◆
◆
◆

Note：The poet Lu You wrote this at the lowest point in his career. He used plum blossoms to express his unyielding and proud character.

5．钱塘湖春行

〔唐〕白居易

孤山寺北贾亭西，水面初平云脚低。

几处早莺争暖树，谁家新燕啄春泥。

乱花渐欲迷人眼，浅草才能没马蹄。

最爱湖东行不足，绿杨阴里白沙堤。

◆
◆
◆
◆

赏：杭州旧称钱塘，钱塘湖即今杭州西湖。此首为白居易描写西湖的经典诗作，其中二、三联为经典名句。诗句生动地演绎了早春的旖旎风光，黄莺、燕子、花草等物象带着春天的气息扑面而来，动静结合，有声有色。"争"与"啄"字极妙，动作显生机；"绿"与"白"色泽清新。"行"而"不足"，诗人对早春西湖和自然风光的无限喜爱跃然纸上。

5. Spring Outing by the Qiantang Lake

By Bai Juyi (772－846 Tang Dynasty)

From north of the Lonely Hill to west of the Jia Pavilion

Low clouds caress the calm lake surface.

A few early orioles squabble over sunny branches;

Newly arrived swallows collect vernal mud for nesting.

Rioting blooms gradually dazzle the eye;

New grass barely covers my horse's hooves.

I love to linger at the lake's eastern shore

Where white embankments lie under willows green.

◆
◆
◆
◆

Note：Bai Juyi served as Governor of Hangzhou from 822

to 824. He was credited with building a dike to regulate water in the West Lake and dredged six clogged community wells in Hangzhou. At that time, the West Lake was still called the Qiantang Lake. The name "West Lake" didn't appear until Bai Juyi addressed this body of water as "West Lake."

6. 少年游·润州作代人寄远

〔北宋〕苏轼

去年相送，余杭门外，飞雪似杨花。 今年春尽，杨花似雪，犹不见还家。

对酒卷帘邀明月，风露透窗纱。 恰似姮娥怜双燕，分明照、画梁斜。

❖
❖
❖
❖

赏：苏轼离开杭州去往润州赈济灾民，冬去春尽离人未归。词中假托爱妻的视角，回忆与现实时空交叠，孤寂思念。飞雪杨花、杨花似雪的比拟，复沓工巧、含蓄深婉。对酒邀月，姮娥双燕，既是伤离之词，又是唯美情诗，表现了夫妻的意真情笃。

6. To the Tune of Youth Outing—A Letter on Behalf of Someone from Runzhou

By Su Shi (1037—1101 Northern Song Dynasty)

Last year we parted

Outside the Yuhang Gate;

Snow drifted like willow fluff.

This year at spring's end

Willow fluff drifts like snow;

You have not returned home.

Wine in hand, I lift the curtain to invite the bright moon in;

Chilly wind seeps through the thin screen.

The tender moon pities the swallow pair

Its bright light

Askew on the painted beam.

❖
❖
❖
❖

Notes：

1. The poet Su Shi makes a subtle complaint in this lyric about his long service time away from home. He wrote this lyric as a woman awaiting her husband's return.

2. Swallows usually make mud nests on beams or under household eaves in spring.

3. Willow floss or fluff，also known as catkins，usually floats like snow in spring when numerous willow trees bloom.

4. Yuhang is the former name of Hangzhou.

7.题灵隐寺山顶禅院

〔唐〕綦毋潜

招提此山顶，下界不相闻。

塔影挂清汉，钟声和白云。

观空静室掩，行道众香焚。

且驻西来驾，人天日未曛。

◆
◆
◆
◆

赏：人们常把綦毋潜的诗和王维的禅诗相提并论。此诗意境高远，富有禅意。禅院建于杭州灵隐寺后北高峰顶，远离尘嚣。经塔在高山之巅，塔影似倒挂于天河。隐约的钟声随白云飘远。禅院静室打坐悟空，寺院外步道上香雾缭绕，渲染着禅寺环境清幽脱俗，不似人间。释氏西来在此驻留点化众生，如日未落。

7. To the Mountain Top Zen Temple Behind the Lingyin Temple

By Qi Wuqian (692—749 Tang Dynasty)

The Zen temple sits on the mountain top

Unknown to the mundane world.

The pagoda's shadow hangs in the Milky Way

Its tolling bell resonating among white clouds.

Meditation on selflessness behind quiet doors

Burning incense permeates the temple paths.

From the west, Buddha descends here;

The sun on earth is yet to be eclipsed.

❖

❖

❖

❖

Note: The Lingyin Temple is not far from the West Lake. It is one of the first Buddhist temples in China dating back to 326.

8. 诉衷情 · 寒食

〔北宋〕仲殊

涌金门外小瀛洲，寒食更风流。 红船满湖歌吹，花外有高楼。

晴日暖，淡烟浮，恣嬉游。 三千粉黛，十二阑干，一片云头。

◆
◆
◆
◆

赏：僧人仲殊身世传奇，曾中进士。早年因放荡不羁被妻子下毒。被救出后弃家为僧，曾寓居杭州宝月寺。寒食节是汉族民间非常重要的传统节日，禁烟火、吃冷食，多祭扫、踏青、蹴鞠等。该词写寒食节西湖特有的热闹盛景。这天杭州晴日柔暖，西湖雾气微蒙，山麓画楼，画船里佳丽欢笑。最后一句从"三千"到"一片"，层层递减，别有一种歌舞散去、身如浮云的生命参悟。

8. To the Tune of Pouring Out Your Heart—

The Cold Food Festival

By Zhong Shu (Northern Song Dynasty)

Beyond the Yongjin Gate is the Isle of Little Yingzhou

Most alluring during the Cold Food Festival.

From painted boats, melodies echo across the lake;

Grand buildings rise above the flowers.

On a warm sunny day

Light mist floats;

People let loose.

Three thousand beautiful women,

Twelve verandas,

One drifting cloud.

◆

◆

◆

◆

Notes:

1. Better known today as the Tomb Sweeping Festival or Qingming Festival, the Cold Food Festival dates back to the 7th century BC, when people refrained from lighting any fires on that day in memory of two hermit sages who perished in a fire.

2. The West Lake's Isle of Little Yingzhou is popular with tourists.

3. The drastic reduction in the final verses creates an inner tension in that the poet believes nothing is perpetual. After all the singing and dancing by the beautiful women abate and wooden verandas crumble, the clouds will always dot the sky.

9.晓出净慈寺送林子方

〔南宋〕杨万里

毕竟西湖六月中，风光不与四时同。

接天莲叶无穷碧，映日荷花别样红。

◆

◆

◆

◆

赏：诗人清晨出寺送友人，路过西湖，见莲叶、荷花水天相接美不胜收。以"毕竟"二字引领全诗，一气贯通。杭州西湖六月风光壮美独特，触目兴叹。荷花娇妍妩媚，碧水映日辽阔壮美。此诗巧用白描、互文和对比手法，诗人对西湖美景的喜爱之情跃然纸上，自然亲切，毫无造作，不愧经典。

9. Bidding Farewell to Lin Zifang outside the Jingci Temple at Dawn

By Yang Wanli (1127—1206 Southern Song Dynasty)

The West Lake in June, looks nonetheless
Different than in any other month.
Endless lotus leaves, a boundless green;
Sun-caressed lotus blossoms, ever so flushed.

◆
◆
◆
◆

Note: As in poem No. 1, this is another of Yang Wanli's
famous poem about the lotus blossoms in the West Lake.

10．暗香·旧时月色

〔南宋〕姜夔

辛亥之冬，予载雪诣石湖。 止既月，授简索句，且征新声，作此两曲，石湖把玩不已，使工妓肄习之，音节谐婉，乃名之曰《暗香》、《疏影》。

旧时月色，算几番照我，梅边吹笛？ 唤起玉人，不管清寒与攀摘。 何逊而今渐老，都忘却春风词笔。 但怪得竹外疏花，香冷入瑶席。

江国，正寂寂，叹寄与路遥，夜雪初积。 翠尊易泣，红萼无言耿相忆。 长记曾携手处，千树压、西湖寒碧。 又片片、吹尽也，几时见得？

◆
◆
◆
◆

赏：姜白石冒雪乘船拜访好友范成大退居的苏州石湖，作《暗香》《疏影》两首新词，取林逋《山园小梅》名句首二字作为新调名。先写梅边月下，笛声悠扬，清景无限的过往旧事；再写而今人已渐老，旧时而今两相对照，更加怀念西湖清寒碧绿和雪后折梅的玉人。"旧时月色"四字破空而来，全诗意味隽永，情思绵邈。

10. To the Tune of Faint Aroma—The Bygone Moonlight

By Jiang Kui（1155—1209 Southern Song Dynasty）

The poet's introduction to the lyric：

In the winter of the Year of Xinhai, I braved snow to visit a friend, a lay Buddhist devotee friend who resides by Stone Lake. At his behest I wrote these lyrics. The lay devotee admired them by reciting them repeatedly. He then summoned his two house songstresses to practice reciting them as well. The melodies and rhythms were sweet and agreeable. I named them as "Faint Aroma" and "Sparse Reflections."

The bygone moon

Cast its light on me numerous times.

Playing my jade flute by the plum blossoms

I awakened a lover with jade-smooth skin.

Bracing against the chill we snapped plum flowers.

Aging like Hexun

I have long neglected my poetry brush.

Remarkably the delicate fragrance of a few plum flowers

Floats from the bamboo grove into the banquet.

The canal towns of Jiangnan

Must now be melancholy.

Sadly it is too far to send you plum blossoms

In evening's drifting snow.

I burst into tears over my green wine cup

In front of the red plum blossoms I think of you.

I will always remember where we were hand in hand;

A thousand plum tree blossom burst

Reflecting on West Lake's blue chilly surface.

Petal by petal

They fade;

When can I see you again?

◆
◆
◆
◆

Note：Jiang Kui's lyrics were among the best in the Song
Dynasty.

11. 山园小梅

〔北宋〕林逋

众芳摇落独暄妍，占尽风情向小园。

疏影横斜水清浅，暗香浮动月黄昏。

霜禽欲下先偷眼，粉蝶如知合断魂。

幸有微吟可相狎，不须檀板共金樽。

◆
◆
◆
◆

　　赏：钱塘人林逋早年浪游晚年归隐，于杭州孤山种梅养鹤，不妻不仕。首联直写山园梅花迎寒风盛开，占尽风情。颔联则是此诗"诗眼"，写绝了梅花幽香超逸的风姿气韵。颈联以拟人手法写白鹤偷眼看梅，粉蝶绕飞也情至销魂。首联直写，颔联传神，颈联拟人，都为烘托尾联作者爱梅之情和幽居之乐。《宋史》称林逋词"澄浃峭特，多奇句"，此诗可见一斑。

11. Small Plum Trees in the Garden

By Lin Bu (circa 967—1028 Northern Song Dynasty)

Others have faded, plum blossoms shine

Enchanting the small garden with all their charm.

Sparse twigs intertwine over a shallow crystal surface;

Faint aromas float under the pale yellow moon.

The white egret glances before perching;

Summer butterflies would be enraptured.

So blessed to share my fondness through poems

No song clappers or wine cups to call for.

❖
❖
❖
❖

Note: Lin Bu was one of the best poets in Chinese literature history，and this poem about plum blossoms is one of his best. His eccentric reclusive lifestyle won him admiration throughout the dynasties. Accompanied only by his red-crowned cranes and a grove of plum blossoms，he refused government positions and lived a solitary life on the Lonely Hill in the West Lake. A plum blossom garden attributed to him on the West Lake's Lonely Hill remains a must-see tourist attraction today. Poem No. 30 is also written by Lin Bu.

12. 浣纱女

〔唐〕王昌龄

钱塘江畔是谁家，江上女儿全胜花。

吴王在时不得出，今日公然来浣纱。

◆
◆
◆
◆

赏：自古江南多佳丽。首句用反诘表达对钱塘女儿的赞美，充满了惊喜和赞叹。随后诗人把笔宕开，将浣纱女与西施相比，对荒淫统治者进行了讽刺。"不得出"与"公然"巧对，还含着诗人对所处世事清平的肯定。全诗语言平实明快却又用意深曲。

12. Washing Girls by the Riverside

By Wang Changling (698—757 Tang Dynasty)

Who resides by the Qiantang River;

Blossoming flowers pale against their daughters' beauty.

Dared not emerge during King Fuchai's reign;

Out and about they come to wash their clothes.

❖
❖
❖
❖

Note: King Fuchai (reigned 495—473 BC) was the last king of the state of Wu who conquered the neighboring state of Yue after a decisive battle. Instead of giving in, the King of Yue drummed up a clever sexpionage plan by sending King Fuchai two beautiful washing girls of Yue, the present day Qiantang

River area，as a tribute with the hope that King Fuchai would
be distracted from his state affairs. The plan was successful and
the King of Yue had his revenge.

13. 杭州春望

〔唐〕白居易

望海楼明照曙霞，护江堤白踏晴沙。

涛声夜入伍员庙，柳色春藏苏小家。

红袖织绫夸柿蒂，青旗沽酒趁梨花。

谁开湖寺西南路，草绿裙腰一道斜。

◆
◆
◆
◆

赏：此诗为白居易任杭州刺史时所作。整首诗用"望"织就了一幅画卷，首联、颔联、颈联一句一景，尾联两句一景，多处景色红绿搭配，远近变换，错落有致。颔联用典写景，将伍员（古音为yun）庙和苏小家融入其中，古今穿梭，"入""藏"两字用得极妙。尾联比喻形象生动。

13. Spring View in Hangzhou

By Bai Juyi (772—846 Tang Dynasty)

The Ocean View Tower bathes in radiant morning glory;

While the white sands glisten along the lake embankments.

Roaring waves echo in Wu Yun's Temple at night;

Spring willows conceal Su Xiao's courtyard.

Delicate hands weave persimmon calyx into silk;

Liquor from taverns summons when pears bloom.

Who built the southwest pass to the lake temple?

A ribbon of green grass askew like a lady's sash.

◆

◆

◆

◆

Note: Please refer to poem No. 5 for information about the poet.

14．长相思

〔南宋〕林升

和风熏，杨柳轻，郁郁青山江水平，笑语满香径。

思往事，望繁星，人倚断桥云西行，月影醉柔情。

◆
◆
◆
◆

赏：林升是南宋诗人，诗文多忧愤，《题临安邸》是其代表作。这首词写景抒情，情景交融。和风杨柳，青山如黛，春景无限。往事如星，西湖断桥，柔情似水。"笑语满香径"极传神，视觉、听觉、嗅觉通感纵贯，一派春景欢乐；"满"与"醉"点化全文，真是君醉柔情我醉诗。

14. To the Tune of Lingering Love Sickness

By Lin Sheng（circa 1163—1189 Southern Song Dynasty）

Gentle breeze soothes；

Arching willow droops.

The calm river meanders along lush green mountains；

Hearty chatter lingers on the fragrant flower pass.

Recall days gone by；

Gazing at a constellation of stars

Leaning against Bridge Duan, the clouds above drift west；

Tender affection arises under the moonlight.

◆
◆
◆
◆

Note: This lyric is credited to Lin Sheng, a poet of the Southern Song Dynasty. Recent research reveals that this is most likely the work of a contemporary poet who used Lin's fame to put this in circulation. This has been a common practice throughout Chinese literary history. The fact that this lyric is readily available on the Internet and collected in many scholarly digital archives attests to its current popularity. Current interest in lyrics demonstrates an ongoing, vigorous interest in the poetic tradition of China.

15. 宿天竺寺晓发罗源

〔唐〕戴叔伦

黄昏投古寺，深院一灯明。

水砌长杉列，风廊败叶鸣。

山云留别偈，王事速归程。

迢递罗源路，轻舆候晓行。

◆
◆
◆
◆

赏：戴叔伦生于隐士之家，入仕期间政绩卓著。中年后上表辞官却客死途中。因曾官居广西容州，故称戴容州。戴有诗论："诗家之景，如蓝田日暖，良玉生烟，可望而不可置于眉睫之前也。"此诗中诗人投宿杭州天竺寺，次日晨起出发前往罗源县。深山古刹，枯叶纷飞。寒灯可亲，山云留别。诗虽看似简练枯澹，实有"象外之象、景外之景"。

15. Lodging at Tianzhu Temple on the Way to Luoyuan

By Dai Shulun (circa 732—789 Tang Dynasty)

Arriving at an ancient temple at dusk

A light shines from deep in the courtyard.

Tall fir trees line the brook;

Fallen leaves rustle in the windy corridor.

The mountain clouds bid farewell Gathas;

Official business interrupts this lingering.

Long and winding is the road to Luoyuan;

My light carriage awaits for dawn departure.

◆
◆
◆
◆

Note: Many ancient Chinese poets took interest in Buddhism.

It was thus fashionable to find lodging at a temple or monastery when traveling. The "lone light" and "rustling fallen leaves" allude to a tranquil world of Zen.

16. 灵隐寺

〔唐〕宋之问

鹫岭郁岧峣，龙宫锁寂寥。

楼观沧海日，门对浙江潮。

桂子月中落，天香云外飘。

扪萝登塔远，刳木取泉遥。

霜薄花更发，冰轻叶未凋。

夙龄尚遐异，搜对涤烦嚣。

待入天台路，看余度石桥。

◆
◆
◆
◆

赏：杭州灵隐寺于东晋建寺，相传因飞来峰为"仙灵所隐"之地，故名"灵隐"。此诗是宋之问贬谪遇赦，回京途中游览灵隐寺所作，一改其宫廷诗风格。鹫岭、龙宫典故自然对仗，"楼观沧海日，门对浙江潮。桂子月中落，天香云外飘"。远近结合，虚实相托，雄壮而又有洒脱出世之意。"霜薄"字妙，"夙龄"律妙，音律协调。以佛教天台宗发源地的天台山度石桥结尾，正衬此时意犹未尽。

16. The Lingyin Temple

By Song Zhiwen (circa 659—712 Tang Dynasty)

The Peak that Flew Hither is lush and jagged

The Buddha's hall holds solitude and silence.

Up in the pavilion, the sun rises from the ocean;

The temple gate faces Zhejiang's tidal bore.

Osmanthus kernels fall from the moon

A heavenly fragrance floating beyond the clouds.

Clutching the vines I reach the upper pagodas;

Before fetching spring water from afar, I split wood.

Thin frosts only spur more flower blooms;

Leaves still unwithered beneath thin ice.

When young, I sought distant scenic spots

To cleanse worldly worries and clamour.

Wait till I step on the road to Mount Tiantai

You will see me cross the stone bridge.

◆
◆
◆
◆

Note：Mount Tiantai is known for its earliest Zen temple in China. A signature stone bridge led to the temple in ancient times.

17. 酒泉子

〔北宋〕潘阆

长忆西湖。尽日凭阑楼上望：三三两两钓鱼舟，岛屿正清秋。

笛声依约芦花里，白鸟成行忽惊起。别来闲整钓鱼竿，思入水云寒。

◆
◆
◆
◆

赏：潘阆性格疏狂，因事亡命，曾隐居钱塘。他有许多写钱塘江的诗词，才情不俗。该词情景交融，先写西湖正清秋的光景，后写回忆者的闲适。词中巧用白描，景中寓情，情以景托，意境悠远高洁，用笔淡炼。结尾与起首自然照应，用笔清闲，情怀逍遥。

17. To the Tune of Ditty from Jiuquan

By Pan Lang（? —1009 Northern Song Dynasty）

West Lake always in my memory.

Leaning all day against the rails upstairs, I gaze afar:

Fishing junks in twos and threes;

The isles are in mid-autumn.

Bamboo flutes whistle faintly among reed floss;

Trails of startled white fowl flap in the air.

Fixing my idle angler's gear

My thoughts are deep with the invigorating lake

Where the clouds and water merge.

◆
◆
◆
◆

Note：Pan Lang was a talented but eccentric lyricist of the Northern Song Dynasty. He wrote a series of lyrics about West Lake and viewing Qiantang tidal bore. He also wrote lyric No. 39.

18. 题临安邸

〔南宋〕林升

山外青山楼外楼，西湖歌舞几时休。

暖风熏得游人醉，直把杭州作汴州。

◆
◆
◆
◆

赏：《宋诗纪事》里记载林升是临安士子，但生卒无考。这是一首"墙头诗"。赵宋王朝偏安汴京，大兴土木，宫殿楼观鳞次栉比。达官巨贾经营宅第，水光山色游人如织。该诗第一句写华丽楼台和靡曼歌舞，描摹了杭州的豪华承平气象。第二句中"熏"与"醉"字极妙，既有游人陶醉之意，也有南宋王朝君臣醉生梦死终至陷落的悲愤之意。

18. Inscribing in a Lodging in Lin'an

By Lin Sheng (circa 1163—1189 Southern Song Dynasty)

Green mountains beyond mountains, mansions after mansions

When will the singing and dancing on West Lake abate?

Comforting breezes intoxicate travelers;

Hangzhou is mistaken for Bianzhou.

◆
◆
◆
◆

Note: Bianzhou (today Kaifeng city) used to be the capital of the Northern Song Dynasty. Hangzhou (known as Lin'an then) was named as a temporary capital after Bianzhou fell into the hands of the Jin Dynasty. The poet was bitter about the fact that people had already forgotten which should be the real capital.

19. 念奴娇·西湖和人韵

〔南宋〕辛弃疾

晚风吹雨，战新荷、声乱明珠苍璧。 谁把香奁收宝镜，云锦红涵湖碧。 飞鸟翻空，游鱼吹浪，惯趁笙歌席。 坐中豪气，看公一饮千石。

遥想处士风流，鹤随人去，已作飞仙伯。 茅舍疏篱今在否，松竹已非畴昔。 欲说当年，望湖楼下，水与云宽窄。 醉中休问，断肠桃叶消息。

❖
❖
❖
❖

赏：这是辛弃疾写西湖初夏美景、借景抒怀的词。上片先写雨打新荷，再喻西湖如香奁宝镜、新荷如初织云锦。"战"与"乱"把雨打新荷仿佛大珠小珠落落玉盘的动态写绝了，真神来之笔；

飞鸟翻空游鱼吹浪的跃动，衬托诗人游兴之高。词的下片缅怀西湖名士林和靖处士风流，实则也是诗人的自我寄怀。此词便是"一饮千石"的辛稼轩豪放与婉约双绝的例证。

19. To the Tune of the Charm of a Maiden Singer——Responding to

Someone's Poem about West Lake

By Xin Qiji（1140—1207 Southern Song Dynasty）

Evening breezes carry rain

Showering against lotus sprouts

Like shining pearls pattering against a green wall.

Who placed the compact back into the fragrant powder box?

Satin clouds and sunset glory over the green lake surface.

Flying birds veer in mid-air;

Fish dart in waves

Trailing after the pleasure boat as they are accustomed to.

Among drinking friends

Admire the one who could drink a thousand cups.

Recalling Lin the Recluse who led a heavenly life

His cranes ascended with him

He who has long been a celestial being.

Where is his thatched hut, sparsely fenced?

The pines and bamboos are not what they used to be.

In bygone years

Under the Lake View Mansion

The sky and lake surface merged as one.

Have another, get tipsy;

Leave the agonizing story of the beautiful Taoye behind.

◆
◆
◆
◆

Note: Xin Qiji was known for his bold and unconstrained style of poetry. This piece shows a mix of boldness as well as gracefulness. The recluse in the second stanza is Lin Bu, who wrote poems No. 11 and No. 30.

20. 望海潮·东南形胜

〔北宋〕柳永

东南形胜，三吴都会，钱塘自古繁华。 烟柳画桥，风帘翠幕，参差十万人家。 云树绕堤沙，怒涛卷霜雪，天堑无涯。 市列珠玑，户盈罗绮，竞豪奢。

重湖叠巘清嘉。 有三秋桂子，十里荷花。 羌管弄晴，菱歌泛夜，嬉嬉钓叟莲娃。 千骑拥高牙，乘醉听箫鼓，吟赏烟霞。异日图将好景，归去凤池夸。

◆
◆
◆
◆

赏：柳永年轻时北上开封应试，经杭州拜谒世谊前辈，便有了这首经典写景投赠词。柳永善写慢词长调，多用铺叙描摹，寓情于景。词从大到小，写尽杭州自然山水与都市豪奢的升平气象。

"三秋桂子"与"十里荷花"的经典意象广为流播,据《鹤林玉露》载,金主亮闻此歌,欣然有慕,遂起投鞭渡江之志。

20. To the Tune of Ocean Tidal Bore Viewing—Blessed Southeast

By Liu Yong (circa 987—1053 Northern Song Dynasty)

Blessed land of the Southeast

The capital city over three Wu dynasties

Qiantang has always been prosperous.

Misty willows over picturesque bridges

Fluttering curtains by green awnings

A hundred thousand residences grand and delicate.

Cloud-wrapped trees dot the sandy riverbanks;

Angry waves roll in white crashes;

The river flows endlessly.

The markets are full of luxurious goods

In households, silk and satin abound;

People flaunt their wealth.

The two lakes flanking distant mountains please the eye.

Osmanthus blooms in mid-autumn

Boundless lotus flowers in summer.

Qiang flutes sound on sunny days;

Melodies for water chestnut picking echo at night;

Children collecting lotus seeds and anglers are joyful.

Soldiers cluster around an official on an outing

Tipsily tapping along with the flutes and drums;

They craft poems about the misty dusk.

Some day I will remember to write this down and

Take pride in telling the folks in the capital.

❖
❖
❖
❖

Note: As a key representative of the Song Dynasty's Graceful and Euphemism School, Liu Yong was the first to reform the Song Dynasty lyrics. With an unsuccessful career，

he spent many of his days with courtesan singers，which greatly

impacted his writing. Legend has it that the heavenly

Hangzhou described in this lyric prompted the leader of the

north to invade the south.

21. 杭州

〔南宋〕谢驿

谁把杭州曲子讴？　荷花十里桂三秋。

那知草木无情物，牵动长江万里愁。

◆
◆
◆
◆

赏：谢驿是南宋福建人，与张栻、张孝祥有交往。唐宋以来讴歌杭州的诗词曲赋不少，西湖荷花、三秋桂子最绝。桂花也是今天杭州的市花。谢驿开篇以自问且自答的方式，概括了杭州的美。但"那知"一句诗情急转，草木本是无情外物，而江南却引发了北人的觊觎与强势侵夺。讴与愁对，伤感悲戚，言简意玄。

21. Hangzhou

By Xie Yi (Southern Song Dynasty)

Who glorified Hangzhou in a lyric?

"That there are ten li of lotus blossoms and osmanthus blooms in autumn."

Grass and trees are insentient beings, yet;

The mighty river worries about enemy crossings.

❖
❖
❖
❖

Note: It was said that after the northern ruler read the lyricist Liu Yong's "To the Tune of Ocean Tidal Bore Viewing—Blessed Southeast" (poem No. 20), he was tempted by the prosperity and unsurpassed natural beauty of Hangzhou, hence in the poem above, innocent lotus blossoms and osmanthus blooms make the Yangtze River worry about an invasion.

22. 忆江南三首

〔唐〕白居易

其一

江南好，风景旧曾谙。

日出江花红胜火，春来江水绿如蓝。

能不忆江南？

其二

江南忆，最忆是杭州。

山寺月中寻桂子，郡亭枕上看潮头。

何日更重游？

其三

江南忆，其次忆吴宫。

吴酒一杯春竹叶，吴娃双舞醉芙蓉。

早晚复相逢？

◆
◆
◆
◆

赏：白居易曾先后任杭州和苏州刺史，江南美景熟稔于心。他在苏州刺史任上写了《答客问杭州》《杭州回舫》等诗，向朋友谈及杭州美景时如数家珍。这组联章诗是诗人奉诏回东都洛阳后所作，看似独立其实贯通完整。月中桂子、枕上潮头和吴酒春茶以及吴娃歌舞等都寄托了切切的思念。

22. Memorable Jiangnan

By Bai Juyi (772−846, Tang Dynasty)

Splendid Jiangnan,

Familiar scenery:

At sunrise, the river's ripples blaze brighter than fire;

In spring, the water is indigo green.

How can I not miss Jiangnan?

Memorable Jiangnan,

Most memorable Hangzhou:

Seeking celestial Osmanthus kernels in the moonlit temple

Leaning against the pavilion, I watch the tidal bore roll in.

When can I return?

Memorable Jiangnan,

Remarkable is the Palace of Wu.

One cup of Wu wine by spring bamboo,

Two Wu dancers mesmerize the hibiscus.

When will I enjoy that again?

◆
◆
◆
◆

Note: Jiangnan, literally "South of the Yangtze River," is known for its rich culture and prosperity. Hangzhou is one of the most important cities of Jiangnan. When the poet served as Hangzhou's governor, he rebuilt a dike in the West Lake, which made Hangzhou an extremely prosperous city.

23．饮湖上初晴后雨

〔北宋〕苏轼

水光潋滟晴方好，山色空蒙雨亦奇。

欲把西湖比西子，淡妆浓抹总相宜。

◆
◆
◆
◆

　　赏：苏轼任杭州通判期间，写了不少吟咏西湖的好诗。此诗从西湖的水色山光入手，写湖上宴游中所见的西湖晴雨姿态。诗人领略了晴方好雨亦奇的景色，把西湖比作淡妆浓抹都极美的西施。自此西子湖成为西湖的别称。好诗往往兴会神到，妙手偶得。

23. Drinking on the Lake with Drizzles after a Short Clearance

By Su Shi (1037—1101 Northern Song Dynasty)

In the sunshine, the lake's surface shimmers after rain;

Steaming drizzle shrouds the mountains in mist.

Compare West Lake and Lady Xizi

The same beauty, bare or blooming.

◆
◆
◆
◆

Note: Xishi was one of the four legendary beauties of ancient China. According to history, while Xishi was washing clothes by a river, she was regarded as so beautiful that she was offered to King Fuchai of Wu by the King of Yue for the latter's diplomatic wooing scheme. King Fuchai was mesmerized by her beauty and neglected his throne, as the King of Yue planned. Two well-known Chinese idioms also are directly related to women's beauty in general in reference to Xishi's beauty specifically: "To sink fish and entice birds to fall; to eclipse the moon and shame flowers." It was said that with or without makeup, Xishi remained beautiful. Thus the poet ingeniously compared West Lake to Lady Xizi (Xishi), gorgeous whether bare in winter or blooming in spring. Poem No. 12 is also based on Xishi's story.

24. 临安春雨初霁

〔南宋〕陆游

世味年来薄似纱，谁令骑马客京华？

小楼一夜听春雨，深巷明朝卖杏花。

矮纸斜行闲作草，晴窗细乳戏分茶。

素衣莫起风尘叹，犹及清明可到家。

◆
◆
◆
◆

赏：此为南宋爱国诗人陆游晚年所作。他在家乡闲居五年后被启用，当时暂居南宋都城临安的西湖附近。首联开篇以问句直抒胸臆，表达世态炎凉和客居京城的心情。颔联和颈联描绘了春雨、杏花、闲作草书、细乳分茶等，也将等候外放期间的一个无聊春日细细道出。"一夜"透露出"京洛多风尘，素衣染成缁"的感慨。尾联宽慰自己清明可到家，诗如叹息。

24. Lin'an after Spring Rain

By Lu You (1125—1210 Southern Song Dynasty)

My enthusiasm for government service is thin as silk；

Why did I ride to the capital to wait command?

Listening to the spring rain in the attic all night

Deep in the alleys tomorrow, people peddle apricot blooms.

Cursive calligraphy flows across scraps of paper；

Fine foamed tea is brewed by the sunny window.

My white scholar's gown untouched by capital dust，

I will be home in time for the Qingming Festival.

Note：In the year of 1186, the poet Lu You was assigned a

low ranking government service position. According to tradition，he had to report to the court for an allocution from the emperor before his term. In boredom at a small lodge waiting to be summoned，he wrote this famous poem about Hangzhou—the capital city of the Southern Song Dynasty.

25.题灵隐寺红辛夷花戏酬光上人

〔唐〕白居易

紫粉笔含尖火焰，红胭脂染小莲花。

芳情乡思知多少，恼得山僧悔出家。

◆
◆
◆
◆

赏：灵隐寺的紫玉兰含苞欲放，形削如笔椎，色艳如红莲。这娇美的花能勾起人们美好的情思，灵隐寺山僧一定后悔出家了吧。灵隐寺住持光上人工于诗，善墨梅，是白居易的好友。这首酬唱诗既打趣了好友，也反衬辛夷花的俏丽动人。

25. Ribbing the Venerable Monk Guang with Red Magnolias at the Lingyin Temple

Bai Juyi (618—907 Tang Dynasty)

Purple buds are sharp fiery flares,

The blush-tinted blooms like small lotus blossoms.

How much affection and nostalgia they spark

Making the monk regret his Buddhist choice.

❖

❖

❖

❖

Note: The Monk Guang was the poet's good friend. As a talented poet himself, Guang often exchanged poems with the poet. Throughout history, Chinese literati frequented temples and monasteries as most of the high monks and nuns were talented poets themselves as well.

26. 重别西湖

〔唐〕李绅

浦边梅叶看凋落，波上双禽去寂寥。

吹管曲传花易失，织文机学羽难飘。

雪欺春早摧芳萼，隼励秋深拂翠翘。

繁艳彩毛无处所，尽成愁叹别溪桥。

❖
❖
❖
❖

赏：李绅是唐代新乐府运动的重要人物，与元稹、白居易交往甚密。因宦海沉浮，诗歌前后期风格有明显的差异。前期继承《诗经》现实主义精神，通俗浅切，以《悯农》为代表；后期向内转，重抒发个人情志，讲究炼字锻句，意境深晦，表现出典雅艳丽的诗歌风格。此诗为后期作品，"雪欺春早""隼励秋深"，寓意深长。

26. Bidding Farewell to West Lake Again

By Li Shen (772—846 Tang Dynasty)

Plum leaves by the lake are ready to fall;

A pair of waterfowls swim deep into solitude.

Flute melodies hasten the fading flowers;

Tapestried wings cannot take flight.

Early spring snow devastated the fragrant blossoms;

A hawk in late fall reassures its wings in green willows.

Dazzling feathers on the lake have all but vanished

With melancholy sighs I part from the bridge.

◆
◆
◆
◆

Notes:

1. Research indicates that Li Shen and the poet Bai Juyi were among the first to use "the West Lake" instead of the Qiantang Lake in their poems.

2. Li Shen was a high ranking official in the Tang Dynasty court. He was involved in partisanship throughout his career. This poem was most likely written when he was at a low point in his life. He expressed his frustration and lamentation throughout.

27. 题磻溪垂钓图

〔唐〕罗隐

吕望当年展庙谟，直钩钓国更谁如。

若教生在西湖上，也是须供使宅鱼。

◆
◆
◆
◆

赏：罗隐是杭州人，在唐末五代时诗名很大，此外散文成就也很高。该诗以姜子牙渭水垂钓、巧遇文王并成就霸业的典故进行古今对照，针砭时弊。五代时，吴越王钱镠规定西湖渔民每天必须交纳若干斤鱼。诗中假设姜子牙生在西湖也难逃此弊政。罗隐诗文多以政治讽刺为题，警当世而戒将来。该诗涉笔成趣，显示了他对现实的批判和讽刺。

27. Responding to the Painting of Angling for Fish at Pan Brook

By Luo Yin (833—910 Tang Dynasty)

Lü Wang strategically demonstrates his lofty ambition;

Who better to capture such talent behind a straight hook?

If Lü Wang were to reside by West Lake today

He wouldn't be exempt from the daily fishing tax.

◆
◆
◆
◆

Notes:

1. Legend says that Lü Wang used a straight fishing hook when fishing in order to spread his fame as a recluse with ambition, as a curved hook would make fishing much easier. King Wen summoned Lü Wang to his court, where he helped

strengthen the kingdom.

2. Fishermen paid a heavy tax at the time. The poet used Lü Wang's anecdote to satirize what he considered a ridiculous tax policy.

28．岳鄂王墓

〔元〕赵孟頫

鄂王墓上草离离，秋日荒凉石兽危。

南渡君臣轻社稷，中原父老望旌旗。

英雄已死嗟何及，天下中分遂不支。

莫向西湖歌此曲，水光山色不胜悲。

❖
❖
❖
❖

赏：有元一代书法家赵孟頫作为宋朝宗室而仕元，其少数诗篇痛惜宋室覆亡，感叹身世之悲。这首七言律诗借凭吊西湖畔岳飞墓而抒百世难解的一腔幽怨。岳坟荒草，萧瑟秋风，肃穆冷峻。历史悲剧令诗人心痛。经历了亡国之痛，诗人满怀愁苦无处说，湖光山色也不胜悲凉。

岳王庙楹联："青山有幸埋忠骨，白铁无辜铸佞臣。"

28. To the Tomb of Yue, the Prince of E

By Zhao Mengfu (1254—1322 Yuan Dynasty)

Grass on the Tomb of Prince of E grows wild;

Stone beasts stand tall in desolate autumn.

The monarch and ministers who crossed south forgot their

kingdom;

Their subjects abandoned in the heartland awaiting soldiers'

banners.

Deep grief follows the fallen hero;

The kingdom hence severed.

Resist singing for the hero by the West Lake;

The lake and mountains are still in unbearable sorrow.

❖
❖
❖
❖

Note：Yue Fei （1103－1142） was a well-known Chinese general of the Southern Song Dynasty. He led several successful counter offensives against the Jin Dynasty in the north. While in hot pursuit following victory after victory，he was summoned back to the court. Yue Fei was put to death on a concocted charge as the emperor feared the defeat of the Jin Dynasty meant the return of the two former emperors in captivity in the north. The Southern Song Dynasty was never able to mount any significant counterattacks after that and subsequently in 1279，Hangzhou fell. Yue Fei was later granted the noble title of Prince E. His shrine still stands by the West Lake to this day.

29. 忆西湖

〔明〕张煌言

梦里相逢西子湖，谁知梦醒却模糊。

高坟武穆连忠肃，添得新祠一座无？

◆
◆
◆
◆

赏：南明儒将张煌言坚持抗清斗争二十多年，被俘后于杭州遇害。其诗文多是在战斗生涯里写成，质朴悲壮，充满强烈的忧国忧民情怀。此诗托物言志，通过梦回西湖追怀抗金将领岳飞的忠义气节。据载张煌言被清兵杀戮前，举目望吴山并发出"大好江山，可惜沦于腥膻！"的叹息。张煌言与岳飞、于谦被后人称为"西湖三杰"。

29. West Lake Recalled

By Zhang Huangyan（1620-1664 Ming Dynasty）

I dreamed I was at West Lake

But the dream blurred after awakening.

The tall tomb of Wumu stands for loyalty.

Will there be a new shrine?

◆
◆
◆
◆

Note：Wumu is the posthumous name of Yue Fei. Please see the note of poem No. 28.

Zhang Huangyan（1620-1664）was a Ming loyalist who served as the defense minister during the reign of the Southern Ming Dynasty. Captured by the soldiers of the Qing Dynasty，he refused to switch sides. He wrote this poem before his execution in Hangzhou.

30．长相思·吴山青

〔北宋〕林逋

吴山青，越山青，两岸青山相对迎，谁知离别情？

君泪盈，妾泪盈，罗带同心结未成，江边潮已平。

◆
◆
◆
◆

赏：在春秋战国时期，钱塘江作为地界，分北吴南越。自古以来，两岸青山见证了无数亲友迎送、生离死别。该词由山水起兴，以第一人称口吻写钱塘江边青年女子送别爱人。罗带还未结成同心，江潮已平，帆船离岸，惜别的人儿早已泪水涟涟。词句回环往复、一唱三叹，令人倍感离情凄凄。

30. To the Tune of Lingering Love Sickness—

Mount Wu Verdant Green

By Lin Bu (967—1028 Northern Song Dynasty)

Mount Wu verdant green,

Mount Yue verdant green,

The river's flanking mountains greet the arriving and departing.

Who knows parting's tender sting?

Your eyes well up;

My eyes well up.

Our silk ribbon truelove knot yet to be tied,

The rivertide is already flat.

◆
◆
◆
◆

Note: Mount Wu (facing Hangzhou) and Mount Yue flank the mighty Qiantang River. The river is known for its spectacular daily tides. A precious window for safe crossing by boats occurred, in ancient times, during flat tides. For lovers separated by the river, their reunions were sweet but nevertheless very short. When the tide is flat, the lovers must part. The poet Lin Bu also was known for his romantic poems. This is one of his masterpieces.

31. 冬至后西湖泛舟看断冰偶成长句

〔唐〕李郢

一阳生后阴飙竭，湖上层冰看折时。

云母扇摇当殿色，珊瑚树碎满盘枝。

斜汀藻动鱼应觉，极浦波生雁未知。

山影浅中留瓦砾，日光寒外送涟漪。

崖崩苇岸纵横散，篙蹙兰舟片段随。

曾向黄河望冲激，大鹏飞起雪风吹。

◆
◆
◆
◆

赏：李郢的诗作多写景状物，风格老练沉郁。这是一首冬至后西湖泛舟的写景状物诗。诗中描写了湖面薄冰漂浮，枯枝散落如珊瑚玉碎。夕照清寒，山影萧瑟。斜照涟漪，游鱼深潜。诗人泛舟湖上，无限陶醉，思绪飞扬。在前文的铺垫下，最后一句与北方壮美雪景的对比，突出西湖冬景优美之至。

31. Boating on West Lake after the Winter Solstice

By Li Ying (Tang Dynasty)

After the Winter Solstice, bone-chilling wind abates;

Ice on the lake starts to crack.

Blue floating glass undulates like fans on the water;

Twigs scatter on the icy lake as shattered coral trees.

Fish know where algae blooms in the side bay;

The geese are numb to the cresting waves.

In the mountain's pale shadow, roof tiles;

Waves ripple in the chilly sunlight.

Tumbling mountain rocks splinter on the reed shore;

A boat pole propels a magnolia canoe.

I've witnessed the mighty crashing waves of the Yellow River

Where drifting snow rages like a giant bird flapping its wings.

❖
❖
❖
❖

Note：The West Lake has different charms throughout the year. This piece describing how the lake in winter looked like to a Tang Dynasty poet more than a thousand years ago is included.

32. 寄西湖林处士

〔北宋〕范仲淹

萧索绕家云，清歌独隐沦。

巢由不愿仕，尧舜岂遗人。

一水无涯静，群峰满眼春。

何当伴闲逸，尝酒过诸邻。

◆
◆
◆
◆

赏：范仲淹曾任杭州知州，当时林和靖已作古二十一年。范仲淹仰慕其风骨，在林逋生前曾两次专程去孤山拜见。此诗通过写西湖边林逋处所的风景表达凭吊与怀念。一水无涯，群峰春色，固然是指西湖孤山的景色。范仲淹把林逋的隐而不仕与尧帝时期的巢父、许由作比，对其旷达闲逸的胸襟表达了十分的倾羡。

32. To Lin the Recluse by West Lake

By Fan Zhongyan (989—1052 Northern Song Dynasty)

Gray clouds circle rooftops;

The secluded hermit chants elegant songs.

Chao and You refused officialdom;

Neither Yao nor Shun was a recluse.

The water here is vast and calm,

Surrounding peaks bloom spring.

What may help pass the time?

Drinking wine with neighbors.

Note:Chao and You were two ancient recluses who refused

officialdom. Yao and Shun were two wise emperors in ancient China. The poet connects between Lin the recluse to Chao and You to glorify Lin's hermitage.

33．西湖竹枝词

〔元〕杨维祯

劝郎莫上南高峰，劝侬莫上北高峰。

南高峰云北高雨， 云雨相催愁杀侬。

◆
◆
◆
◆

赏：诗人杨维祯为元末诗坛领袖，文章巨公，曾携妻儿到杭州
吴山友人处，与好友畅游西湖，深感以往西湖诗作瑰丽风雅居多，
遂创西湖竹枝词九首。他的竹枝词生动俏皮，朗朗上口，开一代
风气之先，后人仿效之作绵绵不绝，直至晚清。此为《西湖竹枝
词》中的第四首，以西湖边南北高峰两两相对，仿刘禹锡的"东边
日出西边雨"，并借用楚襄王和巫山神女云雨高唐的典故，巧妙点
出既甜蜜又令人惆怅的男女之情。

33. West Lake Bamboo Song

By Yang Weizhen (1296—1370 Yuan Dynasty)

Climb not the South Peak, lads;

Climb not the North Peak, girls.

Clouds wrap the south, rain shrouds the north.

Entanglement between the two stings.

◆
◆
◆
◆

Note: Bamboo songs are a type of verse similar to ballads.
The poet Yang Weizhen of the Yuan Dynasty was the first to
write in this style about West Lake while subsequent poets
maintained the tradition throughout the dynasties. "Cloud and

rain" in this ballad，tracing back to ancient lyrics of the Chu

region，implies passionate love between a man and a woman.

34. 杭州送裴大泽赴庐州长史

〔唐〕李白

西江天柱远，东越海门深。

去割慈亲恋，行忧报国心。

好风吹落日，流水引长吟。

五月披裘者，应知不取金。

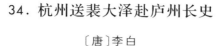

赏：此诗是一首作于杭州的赠别诗。首联写杭州和安徽庐州之间的遥远；颔联颂扬了好友裴大泽割舍亲情、辞亲报国之心；颈联通过落日流水叙写自己触景生情的不舍之情。尾联以五月披裘者作喻，与友共勉为官者清廉不为取金的高洁品行。"五月披裘"典出东汉王充的《论衡·书虚》。这首五律，对仗极工整。

34. Sending Pei Daze to Be the Prefect Governor of Luzhou

By Li Bai (701-762 Tang Dynasty)

The West River is far from Mount Tianzhu;

East Yue is a mouth to the ocean deep.

Tender affections delay departure

With patriotism and benevolence one travels on.

May the good wind extinguish the blazing sun;

The flowing brook hums a farewell song.

For someone wearing a fur coat in May

Knows not to profit from his people.

❖
❖
❖
❖

Note:"Someone in a fur coat in May" refers to a legendary

recluse with a noble mind. The poet Li Bai wrote this in Hangzhou before his friend Pei Daze set off to Prefecture Lu to assume a government position.

35．苏堤春晓

〔清〕阮元

北高峰上月轮斜，十里湖光共一涯。

破晓春天青白色，东风吹冷碧桃花。

❖
❖
❖
❖

赏：月色未尽，曙光初透，湖天一色；乍暖还寒，碧桃报春，天青映衬。远远的北高峰、低垂的月轮和十里湖光如粉彩长卷由远及近，点出"春晓"二字。苏堤是苏轼在任时疏浚西湖用葑泥筑成的，景观久负盛名，南宋时已为西湖十景之首，元时以"六桥烟柳"列入钱塘十景。阮元此诗与聂大年的《苏堤春晓》（见本书第51首）齐名。

35. Spring Dawn on the Su Causeway

By Ruan Yuan (1764—1849 Qing Dynasty)

The full moon hangs atilt on the north peak;

Miles of lake awash in its luminescence.

The spring twilight in azure blue;

A cold easterly wind blows flowering peach blossoms.

◆
◆
◆
◆

Note: "Spring dawn on the Su Causeway" is one of the ten popular tourist hot spots around the West Lake. Its "flowering peach blossoms" have been cultivated as ornamental plants around the West Lake since ancient times.

36. 石壁立招提精舍

〔南朝〕谢灵运

四城有顿踬，三世无极已。

浮欢昧眼前，沉照贯终始。

壮龄缓前期，颓年迫暮齿。

挥霍梦幻顷，飘忽风雷起。

良缘迨未谢，时逝不可俟。

敬拟灵鹫山，尚想祇洹轨。

绝溜飞庭前，高林映窗里。

禅室栖空观，讲宇析妙理。

◆
◆
◆
◆

赏：杭州灵隐寺有三生石，谢灵运幼时曾寄养于灵隐寺，成年后与高僧交往密切。其山水诗中常融入佛教思想，这首《石壁立招提精舍》便是一例。三生源于佛教因缘，即前世、今生和来世。谢灵运以佛教四门游观开篇，引出三生轮回无涯，慨叹人世浮欢如镜花水月，流年飞逝。其中"绝溜飞庭前，高林映窗里"为山水诗名句。

36. On the Completion of a Cliffside Buddhist Dwelling

By Xie Lingyun (385—433 Southern Dynasties)

The four sights reveal conditioned existence;

The past, present and future ever rotate.

Worldly pleasures amuse the eye;

Let mindfulness prevail.

Time slips idly by in youth;

Gray-haired you lament its passing.

Distorted dreams do not linger,

Nor do wind and thunder persist.

Seize the opportunity to immerse in Dharma;

Time wasted is forever lost.

I yearn for the Griddahakuta Hill.

I wish to worship at Jeta's Grove.

A stream cascades beyond the courtyard;

Tall woods fill the temple window.

The meditation room proffers insight into selflessness;

The master's teaching illuminates the wondrous doctrines.

◆

◆

◆

◆

Note: "The stone of the past, present and future" is located outside of the Lingyin Temple. It became a sought-after attraction after the 2017 popular TV series under the name *Eternal Love*, based on the legend of this stone.

37. 杭州开元寺牡丹

〔唐〕张祜

浓艳初开小药栏，人人惆怅出长安。

风流却是钱塘寺，不踏红尘见牡丹。

◆
◆
◆
◆

赏：诗人早年寓居苏州，常往来于扬州、杭州等地，后来入长安，仕途坎坷，转而隐居，模山范水题咏名寺，诗作流传不少。这首诗写艳丽的牡丹初开，人们都争相出都城长安观赏。第二句笔锋一转，怀念杭州开元寺内的牡丹，不出寺门就能欣赏。张祜曾隐居多年，"不踏红尘"一句也透露出诗人坎坷不达以布衣终的逍遥自得心境。长安、洛阳牡丹固然闻名，杭州牡丹盛况其实也已逾千年，宋代诸多诗人都有题写。苏轼的《牡丹记叙》一文便记录了当年杭州官民同赏牡丹的盛会。

37. The Moutans of the Kaiyuan Temple in Hangzhou

By Zhang Hu (785—849 Tang Dynasty)

Bright-colored moutans blossom in the small garden;

Everyone hopes to rush from Chan'an for a glimpse.

The Qiantang Temple is most charming;

Its moutan blossoms unknown to the mundane world.

◆
◆
◆
◆

Note: Moutans usually grow the best in Chang'an and Luoyang in the north. The poet wrote about the flourishing moutans in the Qiantang Temple of Hangzhou; even folks in capital Chang'an were tempted to journey a long way for a glimpse.

38．与从侄杭州刺史良游天竺寺

〔唐〕李白

挂席凌蓬丘，观涛憩樟楼。

三山动逸兴，五马同遨游。

天竺森在眼，松风飒惊秋。

览云测变化，弄水穷清幽。

叠嶂隔遥海，当轩写归流。

诗成傲云月，佳趣满吴洲。

❖
❖
❖
❖

赏：这是李白到杭州与从侄、时任杭州刺史的李良同游天竺寺的所见所感。当时的西湖（钱塘湖）还只是一个浅水湾。在白居易等疏浚古井、治理钱塘湖后，尤其是苏轼到任杭州之后，诗文流播，杭州始成东南名都。这里的天竺寺是今天的下天竺寺。下天竺寺，在杭州府城西十五里，建于晋代，寺前后有飞来、莲花诸峰,合涧、跳珠诸泉,梦谢、流杯、月桂诸亭,游人多至其间。"诗成傲云月"颇显盛唐气象,是李白诗歌风格的标识,真可谓"李杜文章在,光焰万丈长"。

38. A Visit to Tianzhu Temple with My Nephew Liang the Governor of Hangzhou

By Li Bai (701—762 Tang Dynasty)

Hoisting my sail I come to this paradise

Admiring the tidal bore from the tower above.

My enthusiasm surges like the cresting water;

Five horses accompany us on a tour.

The grand Tianzhu Temple is within sight;

Melodies through the pines announce approaching autumn.

Trace the changing clouds above;

Follow the streams to their trickling fountainheads.

An ocean is far over the mountains;

The river rolls on outside my window.

The moon and clouds pale against my poem's glory;

The scenery of Wu brings endless joy.

◆
◆
◆
◆

Note: The Tianzhu Temple is one of several near the famous Lingyin Temple. Li Bai or Li Po in earlier translations, was one of the greatest Tang Dynasty poets lauded as "the poet with celestial talent."

39. 酒泉子

〔北宋〕潘阆

长忆西山，灵隐寺前三竺后，冷泉亭上旧曾游，三伏似清秋。

白猿时见攀高树，长啸一声何处去？ 别来几向画阑看，终是欠峰峦！

◆
◆
◆
◆

赏：该词是对杭州西山的回忆。起句定位西山，三竺寺是指上、中、下天竺寺。白居易与三竺寺结缘甚深，留下许多诗篇。上片写西山古木参天，幽静凉爽；下片以白猿攀树、长啸声远，写西山的道佛灵气。最后以一"欠"字反衬灵隐山峰峦之美。该词采用白描、留白、反衬等手法写西山的清幽神奇，自然美感。

39. To the Tune of Ditty from Jiuquan

By Pan Lang (? —1009 Northern Song Dynasty)

The memorable West Mountains

In front of the Lingyin Temple, behind the three Tianzhu

monasteries.

In the Cold Spring Pavilion I left my footprints

Amid mid-summers like cool autumn.

The white monkey is often spotted climbing tall trees.

To where does it disappear after a long howl?

I often revisit the mountains in paintings;

The brushed peaks do not compare at all.

❖
❖
❖
❖

Note：Please refer to poem No. 17 for more information about the poet.

40. 谒岳王墓

〔清〕袁枚

江山也要伟人扶，神化丹青即画图。

赖有岳于双少保，人间才觉重西湖。

◆
◆
◆
◆

赏：此诗出句不凡，一语双关。"江山也要伟人扶"，既可以看作自然山水需文人添彩，也可以看作江山社稷需伟人扶持。西湖本身美景如画，加上岳飞和于谦的祠庙和坟墓，更使世人看重。明代诗人张煌言诗云："日月双悬于氏墓，乾坤半壁岳家祠"，展现了世人的景仰之情。

40. Pay Respects to the Yue Fei Temple

By Yuan Mei (1716—1797 Qing Dynasty)

Rivers and mountains, too, benefit from a great personage;

Nature's superb artistry paints the land.

Because of Deputy Marshal Yue and Yu

The West Lake earns all our respect.

◆
◆
◆
◆

Notes:

1. See the note of poem No. 28.

2. Yu Qian (1398−1457), born in Hangzhou, played an

important role in 1449, defending Beijing from an invasion.

He was later appointed by the new emperor as the crown

prince's guardian and tutor. In 1457, after the former emperor was released from captivity, he returned to Beijing. In a coup the former emperor regained power and executed Yu Qian on false charges of treason. Yu Qian was posthumously rehabilitated by subsequent emperors who built shrines in his honor in Beijing and Hangzhou.

41. 谢龙井僧献秉中寄茶

〔明〕刘邦彦

春茗初收谷雨前，老僧分惠意勤虔。

也知顾渚无双品，须试吴山第一泉。

竹里细烹清睡思，风前小啜悟诗禅。

相酬拟作长歌赠，浅薄何能继玉川？

❖
❖
❖
❖

赏：西湖龙井茶是中国十大名茶之一，讲究采摘时间，以春茶为贵。谷雨前采制的叫"雨前茶"。自古便有"雨前是上品"的说法。该诗将茶、诗、禅融合，体现了龙井茶文化融合山寺、泉湖、诗禅于一体的特色。

41. In Appreciation of the Dragon Well Green Tea

Shared by a Monk

By Liu Bangyan (Ming Dynasty)

Spring tea is picked before the Grain Rain;

The senior monk humbly shared some with me.

The tea from Guzhu is unrivaled

Brewed with the best of Mount Wu's spring water.

Several steeps in the bamboo grove lift torpor;

In the breeze, each sip elucidates Zen poetry.

I wish to write a long poem in return for his generosity

But with my limited talent I stop short.

❖
❖
❖
❖

Note: In the Jiangnan region of China, the farmer's almanac states "no snow after Qingming, and no frost after Guyu." Guyu, literary means Grain Rain (the rain which nurtures the sprouts of hundreds of grains), marking not only the time for planting, but also harvesting for tea. Green tea picked before the Grain Rain is most tender and savory. Dragon Well Green Tea of Hangzhou is generally considered one of the best in China.

42．春题湖上

〔唐〕白居易

湖上春来似画图，乱峰围绕水平铺。

松排山面千重翠，月点波心一颗珠。

碧毯线头抽早稻，青罗裙带展新蒲。

未能抛得杭州去，一半勾留是此湖。

◆
◆
◆
◆

赏：开篇似鸟瞰图，西湖春日风景如画。此后具体绘景，却跳出常见的山水描述，看到农作物早稻，关怀民情。将早稻以比喻诗化。早稻似碧毯线头，新蒲似青罗裙带。后两句抒情，对杭州的不舍之意，"一半勾留"是因为西湖。此诗作于诗人卸任杭州刺史前夕。该诗情景交融，是描绘西湖景色的名篇之一。

42. Spring on the Lake

By Bai Juyi (772—846 Tang Dynasty)

Spring turns the lake into a master's canvas;

Jagged peaks circle the calm water surface.

Pines cover the mountains with a thousand layers of green;

The full moon rests in ripples like a shining pearl.

On the green carpet early rice shoots are budding;

Tender cattails unfurl like the hem of a silk skirt.

I am reluctant to leave Hangzhou behind

This lake is half of my yearning.

◆
◆
◆
◆

Note: The poet Bai served as governor of Hangzhou for two years. He left many marvelous poems about the West Lake.

43．余杭

〔南宋〕范成大

春晚山花各静芳，从教红紫送韶光。

忍冬清馥蔷薇酽，薰满千村万落香。

❖
❖
❖
❖

赏：范成大与杨万里、陆游、尤袤合称南宋"中兴四大诗人"。其诗风格平易浅显、清新妩媚。其诗题材广泛，尤其以写乡村社会生活内容的作品成就最高。这首《余杭》写暮春时节杭州近郊山野的美丽风光，山花烂漫，群花争艳。然而诗人并不为春花凋零伤感，反用"从教"二字，任凭春花凋谢送走美丽的时光。忍冬与蔷薇平凡朴素，入诗则富有乡间情趣，足见诗人的闲适自然，恬淡优雅，蕴含禅意。

43. Yuhang

By Fan Chengda（1126—1193 Southern Song Dynasty）

Mountain flowers quietly bloom at spring nightfall;

The red and purple will again, initiate the end of glory.

Honeysuckle's aroma is delicate, rose's intense;

Their fragrance permeates a thousand villages and neighborhoods.

◆
◆
◆
◆

Note: This is one of Fan Chengda's Zen poems. Yuhang is the former name of Hangzhou.

44．余杭形胜

〔唐〕白居易

余杭形胜四方无，州傍青山县枕湖。

绕郭荷花三十里，拂城松树一千株。

梦儿亭古传名谢，教妓楼新道姓苏。

独有使君年太老，风光不称白髭须。

◆
◆
◆
◆

赏：白居易于长庆二年至四年（822—824）任杭州刺史，与杭州结下深厚情谊。除了筑堤修井为民谋福外，他还写了许多推广余杭的诗歌。此诗先写杭州傍山枕湖，西湖荷花、九里云松、灵隐山上的梦谢亭和歌伎苏小小的传奇都为余杭增添了不少魅力。最后诗人戏谑调侃，发出了余杭美好而我已老的感慨。

44. Splendid Yuhang

By Bai Juyi (772—846 Tang Dynasty)

Splendid Yuhang is surpassed by nowhere else

Residing by green mountains and resting by the lake.

Lotus blossoms circle the outskirts for thirty li;

A thousand pines cluster in the city corner.

The Meng'er Pavilion is famous for the poet Xie;

Su the courtesan resides in a new pleasure house.

Only the governor himself is aged;

His gray mustache dull against the surroundings.

❖
❖
❖
❖

Note: Bai Juyi oversaw Hangzhou in 822. He wrote this

poem to extol his surroundings for self-amusement. Courtesan Su first appeared in this poem, after which subsequent poems and lyrics referred to her often.

45．余杭四月

〔元〕白珽

四月余杭道，一晴生意繁。

朱樱青豆酒，绿草白鹅村。

水满船头滑，风轻袖影翻。

几家蚕事动，寂寂昼门关。

◆
◆
◆
◆

赏：诗人白珽长于描绘秀丽自然风光与田园生活。人间四月的杭州，春光明媚，生机盎然。朱樱、青豆、绿草、白鹅，好一幅清新画卷，色泽相衬。春水涌动，船儿荡漾，微风拂衣。家家户户忙蚕事，闭门不出免冲撞。此诗描绘了丝绸之府杭州的春日美景、重蚕习俗。孵蚕期间，农家关闭大门，贴以"蚕月知礼"的红纸防生人闯入，"开蚕门"则是当地隆重的节日。

45. Yuhang in April

By Bai Ting (1248—1328 Yuan Dynasty)

Yuhang in the fourth lunar moon

All things teem with life under the sun.

Red cherries and wine shared over green soya;

Lush grass and white geese pervade the villages.

A boat sails smoothly on the full river;

Gentle breezes flutter my sleeves.

It is the silkworm spinning season;

Many doors shut tight in broad daylight.

❖
❖
❖
❖

Note: It is a tradition during silkworm season for households to shut their front doors so outsiders won't intrude，as superstitiously

they might bring bad luck and cause a reduction in silk.

46.人月圆·春晚次韵

〔元〕张可久

萋萋芳草春云乱，愁在夕阳中。 短亭别酒，平湖画舫，垂柳骄骢。

一声啼鸟，一番夜雨，一阵东风。 桃花吹尽，佳人何在，门掩残红。

◆
◆
◆
◆

赏:这是一首春日送别的小令。上片实写西湖边芳草夕阳、平湖短亭的送别场景,垂柳白马,画面感极强。下片写离恨绵绵,叠用三个量词,对偶巧妙,音律上亦造成反复咏叹、回肠荡气的效果。三种声音再三催促才惊醒沉醉在回忆中的词人,足见沉湎眷念之深。最后三句揭示故地重游的惆怅。此词情景交融,清新工整。

46. To the Tune of a Reunion under the Full Moon—Spring Evening

By Zhang Kejiu (circa 1270—1350 Yuan Dynasty)

Lush grass sways, spring clouds drift;

The setting sun glows despondent.

Farewell wine is poured at the Five Li Pavilion;

Painted boats float on a calm lake;

Handsome piebald horses rest under arching willows.

A bird's caw,

A night's drizzle,

An easterly breeze.

The peach blossoms have all blown away.

Where is the beautiful woman?

A half shut door encloses the faded red blooms.

◆
◆
◆
◆

Note：Five Li Pavilion，also known as "a short distance pavilion，" is a resting place in ancient times，usually about 2. 5 km from a city. A Ten Li Pavilion is considered "a long distance pavilion. "

47．登飞来峰

〔北宋〕王安石

飞来山上千寻塔，闻说鸡鸣见日升。

不畏浮云遮望眼，自缘身在最高层。

◆
◆
◆
◆

赏：诗人王安石在浙江鄞县知县任满回江西临川故里时，途经杭州，写下此诗。此诗绘景抒怀，写景寄情，深藏哲理，借登飞来峰展现壮志与抱负。以"千寻"喻山塔之高，见旭日东升之壮阔。以"不畏"的壮语，体现了心怀改革大志、敢于斗争的精神。"浮云蔽日"如"邪臣蔽贤"，正如汉·陆贾在《新语·慎微》中所言："故邪臣之蔽贤，犹浮云之障日月也。"诗句最后形象地揭示了登高能望远的道理。

47. Ascending the Peak that Flew Hither

By Wang Anshi (1021—1086 Northern Song Dynasty)

The tall pagoda sits on the Peak that Flew Hither;

People say you can see sunrise at rooster's crow.

Worrying not about drifting clouds blocking the view

You are at the summit of all things.

◆
◆
◆
◆

Note: Wang Anshi was a well-known poet, statesman and reformist. He wrote this poem at the pinnacle of his career as prime minister in the Song Dynasty court in charge of a nationwide reform. He demonstrated his resolve and determination in this poem.

48．左顾保叔塔右顾雷峰塔并南北高峰塔为四

〔元〕方回

四山角立四浮屠，绝似双林竞宝珠。

万古一丸拿不去，夜深朗月浸澄湖。

◆
◆
◆
◆

赏：方回是元代诗人、诗论家。保叔塔（也称保俶塔）、雷峰塔、南北高峰塔，四塔矗立，西湖在其中。"竞"字巧妙，似竞争宝珠的青睐。无人能带走西湖，夜深朗澈的月光沐浴其中。"万古一丸拿不去"，蕴含了"人生如浮云，霜天不曾更"的禅意。

48. Looking Left at the Baochu Pagoda and Right at the Leifeng Pagoda with Two Other Pagodas of the North and South Peaks

By Fang Hui (1227—1305 Yuan Dynasty)

Four pagodas stand, on four cardinal mountains

As if contending for the precious jewel's favor.

No one can ever steal this crystal lake;

Deep at night, the bright moon bathes in it.

◆
◆
◆
◆

Note: There are four pagodas on the four sides of the West Lake, as if each is vying for the lake's attention. The poet included some Zen thoughts in the last two lines.

49．题杭州樟亭

〔唐〕郑谷

漠漠江天外，登临返照间。

潮来无别浦，木落见他山。

沙鸟晴飞远，渔人夜唱闲。

岁穷归未得，心逐片帆还。

◆
◆
◆
◆

赏：郑谷为唐末诗人，僖宗年间进士，诗文讲究遣词炼句，风格清浅婉约，浅白易懂。颔联"潮来无别浦，木落见他山"为名句，在众多观潮诗中脱颖而出，用潮涨而彼岸消隐来反衬钱塘江大潮的壮观。江潮过后，两岸平静如初，诗人从沙鸟翻飞、渔人夜唱中联想到自己孤身在外漂泊，岁末未得归，思乡之情油然而生，过渡自然，不着痕迹。

49. Ascending the Zhang Pavilion

By Zheng Gu (circa 851−910 Tang Dynasty)

The river and sky are vast and endless;

I come to ascend at sunset.

The tidal bore confounds the river and ocean;

Fallen leaves reveal distant mountains.

Beach birds fly far on sunny days;

Fishermen hum ballads at night.

At year's end wandering still

My heart is with that distant sail homeward bound.

◆
◆
◆
◆

Note: In the Tang Dynasty, the Zhang Pavilion by the Qiantang River was famous for tidal bore watching.

50. 送公仪龙图知杭州

〔北宋〕梅尧臣

在昔汉中微，我祖入吴门。

公今领名都，千骑拥高轩。

与古异出处，素节古本原。

江观白马潮，水花长鲸奔。

山飘月桂子，天香一国繁。

壮奇巳若此，纤侈尚亦存。

旧闻其风俗，色易而柔温。

太守朝驾车，闾巷焚兰荪。

太守暮还府，灯烛照旗旛。

清歌延冠盖，广湖浮酒樽。

成都与余杭，天下莫比论。

彼为公故乡，此为公偃藩。

吏民宜寡事，恺悌有谣言。

赏：梅尧臣与苏舜钦齐名，时号"苏梅"。梅尧臣为北宋现实主义诗人，有"宋诗开山祖"之誉，其诗擅长"状难写之景如在目前，含不尽之意见于言外"。此诗写实、平淡、含蓄。诗中公仪龙图是指梅挚。梅挚，字公仪，北宋成都府新繁县人，龙图阁学士。诗人提到杭州的美景及民众亲善守礼，末尾勉励好友在任上多行黄老之道，则必会得到百姓的赞扬。

50. Sending Gongyi the Court Scholar to Assume Governorship in Hangzhou

By Mei Yaochen（1002—1060 Northern Song Dynasty）

When the heartland was war-torn

Our ancestors migrated to Wu.

You will soon govern a famous prefect

A thousand horses and tall flags trailing you.

Though the prefect is far from the central plain

Its customs and traditions are of the same root.

By the river you will be awed by the tidal bore

Like giant whales surging in competition.

Osmanthus blossoms fall in the mountains;

Heavenly fragrance permeates a land of abundance.

Its scenery spectacular and marvelous;

Elegance and luxury coexist.

I have long heard of its traditions

Of friendly people and polite manners.

Before the governor's morning visit

Incense will infuse streets and alleys.

After the governor's return at dusk

Lights will illuminate his soldiers' banners.

Cappellas envelop your carriage;

Wine is served on a vast lake.

Chengdu and Yuhang are

Unsurpassed earthly twin prefects.

The former, your birth place;

The latter, your service post.

Free your subjects from bondage;

Paeans will resound throughout your prefect.

◆
◆
◆
◆

Note：Mei Yaochen was a great realistic poet and a pioneer of the "new subjective" poetry style of the Song Dynasty. In the vein of the Chinese literati tradition to write poems for every occasion，Mei wrote this piece before his friend's departure to Hangzhou to assume governorship.

51. 苏堤春晓

〔明〕聂大年

树烟花雾绕堤沙，楼阁朦胧一半遮。

三竺钟声催落月，六桥柳色带栖鸦。

绿窗睡觉闻啼鸟，绮阁妆残唤卖花。

遥望酒旗何处是，炊烟起处有人家。

◆
◆
◆
◆

赏：聂大年为明中叶制曲大家，其诗名直追梅尧臣，西湖边的百寿亭就因为他的诗句"塔影亭亭引碧流"而更名为亭亭亭。聂大年因仕途不顺而鲜有意气风发之作。诗的首联为《苏堤春晓》的经典名句，随后便是三竺寺梵钟入耳。写的是春晓，却不见黄莺而见栖鸦。"绮阁妆残唤卖花"句与其名篇《卜算子·杨柳小蛮腰》中的"忙整玉搔头"颇为相似，年长色衰的女子与失意文人一样强打精神，所谓人如落花。末联透露出不如"青旗沽酒趁梨花"的惆怅意绪。

51. Spring Dawn on the Su Causeway

By Nie Danian（1402—1456 Ming Dynasty）

Foggy trees and misty blooms circle the causeway

Indistinct mansions half in shade.

The tolls from Tianzhu temples urge the moon to descend；

The willows of the six arched bridges harbor nesting crows.

Birds disrupt my nap by the green window；

In fading makeup, I call for a flower peddler from my veranda.

Searching the horizon for a wine tavern's pennant；

There！ Where smoke rises from a chimney.

◆
◆
◆
◆

Note：Nie Danian was a talented poet with an unsuccessful

career. He often used the image of a songstress or dancer whose beauty is fading (reference of "fading makeup" above) to lament that he hadn't achieved anything in life. A wine tavern's pennant promises some solace at poem's conclusion.

52．贺新郎·兵后寓吴

〔南宋〕蒋捷

深阁帘垂绣。 记家人、软语灯边，笑涡红透。 万叠城头哀怨角，吹落霜花满袖。 影厮伴、东奔西走。 望断乡关知何处，羡寒鸦、到著黄昏后。 一点点，归杨柳。

相看只有山如旧。 叹浮云、本是无心，也成苍狗。 明日枯荷包冷饭，又过前头小阜。 趁未发、且尝村酒。 醉探枵囊毛锥在，问邻翁、要写牛经否。 翁不应，但摇手。

❖
❖
❖
❖

赏：蒋捷为宋末四大家之一，词风"洗炼缜密，语多创获"。元兵攻破临安后，词人漂泊平江府，其间所作之词多哀怨悱恻。此词以日常景物衬托词人亡国后的颠沛辛酸，又用记忆中故乡杭城的温馨画面反衬现实中的怨角、霜花、寒鸦及荷包冷饭，感慨国破家亡之后，人不如鸦的境遇。末句的手抄牛经无人问，也间接反映了战后农业生产的凋敝。其现实主义手法在抒情体宋词中不可多得！

52. To the Tune of Rejoicing over Recent Refreshing Air—Dwelling

in Wu after the Fall of the Southern Song Dynasty

By Jiang Jie（1245—1305 Southern Song Dynasty）

Embroidered screens conceal a boudoir.

Recalling my family，

Speaking softly by a light

Dimples on blushed cheeks.

Lamenting horns resonate over the city wall

Showering frost crystals onto my sleeves.

Wandering alone，

I drift from pillar to post.

Where is my hometown?

I admire crows in the chilly air；

After sundown

One by one

They return to a willow tree.

Only the mountains remain as they were.

A sigh to the drifting clouds

Which aimlessly

Transform into gray dogs.

Tomorrow I will bring cold rice wrapped in a dried lotus leave

And pass the small distant hill.

Before setting off

Why not try some local rice wine?

Drunk, I reach into my sack for a brush

And ask the old farmer next to me

Would he like the "Water Buffalo Book" copied.

The farmer remains silent,

Shakes his head.

❖
❖
❖
❖

Note: A talented poet, Jiang Jie was a high-ranking official in the Southern Song Dynasty. After the Southern Song Dynasty fell, he refused to serve. Like many other Song loyalists, he then had to roam "from pillar to post." This poem faithfully reflects the chaos in Hangzhou after the demise of the Southern Song Dynasty.

53. 题杭州孤山寺

〔唐〕张祜

楼台耸碧岑，一径入湖心。

不雨山长润，无云水自阴。

断桥荒藓涩，空院落花深。

犹忆西窗月，钟声在北林。

◆
◆
◆
◆

赏：白居易与诗人张祜相遇，与他同游西湖和孤山。张祜留恋景物，遂写下此诗。孤山寺原在杭州西湖边孤山上。诗人写孤山寺，从空间、气候、风物等方面描绘，显其幽静，以静写静，其中"不雨山长润，无云水自阴"历为名家称道。尾联突破，"忆"颇具匠心，虚实结合，西窗外的月亮在记忆中闪耀。以声写静，钟声在林中回荡，更显清幽旷远。

53. The Lonely Hill Temple of Hangzhou

By Zhang Hu（circa 785－849 Tang Dynasty）

Towers stand on a verdant hill；

One path leads to the distant isle in the lake.

The surrounding mountains ever moist without rain；

Its water cool even on cloudless days.

Broken Bridge is covered with thick green moss；

Fading flower petals accumulate in vacant courtyards.

The moon outside the western window shines bright in memory；

Bell tolls resonate deep in the north woods.

◆
◆
◆
◆

Note：The Lonely Hill is a major tourist attraction in the

West Lake. No temple remains on the hill today. This piece unfurls a scroll of the Lonely Hill in the Tang Dynasty.

54．蟾宫曲

〔元〕奥敦周卿

西湖烟水茫茫。 百顷风潭，十里荷香。 宜雨宜晴，宜西施淡抹浓妆。 尾尾相衔画舫，尽欢声无日不笙簧。 春暖花香，岁稔时康。 真乃上有天堂，下有苏杭。

◆
◆
◆
◆

赏：这是奥敦周卿歌咏杭州西湖的两首小令中的一首，生动地表达了诗人对西湖的依依不舍之情。词中罗列了雨中西湖、十里风荷、平湖画船等景致，也写了西湖春暖花开、杭州四季安康的富足。该作借用苏轼、范成大等人的诗句，对西湖所在的江南的美丽与富足表达赞叹。

54. To the Tune of the Melody from the Moon Palace

By Audun Zhouqing (Yuan Dynasty)

Misty West Lake's water is vast.

A hundred acres of rippling surface

Ten li of lotus fragrance.

In sun or rain, like Lady Xishi

Charming whether natural or adorned.

Painted pleasure boats sail in succession;

Happy laughter aboard;

Not a day goes without strings and pipes.

Warm spring scented with fragrant blooms,

Peace and prosperity abound.

Indeed "Paradise in heaven,

Suzhou and Hangzhou on Earth."

◆
◆
◆
◆

Note："Paradise in heaven，Suzhou and Hangzhou on Earth" first appeared in poet Fan Chengda's writings（author of poem No. 43）. This is now a well-established saying.

55．生查子·元夕

〔北宋〕欧阳修

去年元夜时，花市灯如昼。 月上柳梢头，人约黄昏后。

今年元夜时，月与灯依旧。 不见去年人，泪湿春衫袖。

◆
◆
◆
◆

赏：这是一首清切婉丽、别具一格的小词。元宵节自唐玄宗开元时起，以三天灯火烟花秀为主。至宋代延长为"五夜元宵"的风俗，词人也多以此为题。此词今昔对比，有崔护"人面不知何处去"的伤感。语言看似平淡，实则风味隽永。词人于杭州官巷口喧闹的元宵之夜触景生情，情不能已。平淡入妙，是宋词里的抒情上品。

55. To the Tune of Sprouting Season Ditty—The Lantern Festival

By Ouyang Xiu（1007—1072 Northern Song Dynasty）

Last year at the Lantern Festival

Lights at the ornament market shined bright as day.

The moon climbed just above the willow tree；

We set a sweet date for nightfall.

This year at the Lantern Festival

The moon and lights shine as usual.

My lover is nowhere to be seen；

Tears dampen my thin spring sleeve.

◆
◆
◆
◆
◆

Note：Many scholars now believe the poetess Zhu Shuzhen wrote this，not Ouyang Xiu. It was not uncommon at the time for a lesser known poet or poetess to use a well-known name to get his/her poems recorded in history. The theme and style is similar to Zhu's poem（poem No. 68）and lyric（poem No. 69）in this collection.

56．住西湖白云禅院作此

苏曼殊

白云深处拥雷峰，几树寒梅带雪红。

斋罢垂垂浑入定，庵前潭影落疏钟。

◆
◆
◆
◆

赏：苏曼殊为清末民初奇才，通晓英、日、梵语，可惜英年早逝，葬于西湖边。苏曼殊短短一生中曾多次出家，此诗便是在雷峰塔下的西湖白云禅寺出家时所作。"雷峰如老衲，保俶似美人"，雷峰塔被万千白云簇拥，云动塔不动；雪欺早梅，而"春风自有期，桃李乱春坞"，一"拥"一"带"实是千炼万锤之词，禅意满满。斋罢观空打坐，寺外疏钟落三潭，犹如綦毋潜的"塔影挂清汉，钟声和白云"及王维的"唯有白云外，疏钟闻夜猿"。无形无相无执的钟声既警世又出世，让人顿感空灵脱俗，实为禅诗佳作！

56. Lodging at West Lake's White Cloud Zen Temple

By Su Manshu (1884－1918)

Deep in white clouds, Leifeng Pagoda stands;

A few plum trees bloom red under snow's cover.

After a vegetarian meal I sink into a mindless trance.

Intermittent bell tolls descend on pools facing the temple.

◆
◆
◆
◆

Note: Manshu was a gifted, but short lived poet. This is one of his beautiful Zen poems written while lodging at the White Cloud Zen Temple near Leifeng Pagoda, which is not far from the famous spot—Three Pools Mirroring the Moon in the West Lake. The standing pagoda in relation to drifting clouds, blooms in winter and tolling bells help create an inviting Zen atmosphere.

57．甲辰八月辞故里

〔明〕张煌言

国破家亡欲何之，西子湖头有我师。

日月双悬于氏墓，乾坤半壁岳家祠。

惭将赤手分三席，敢为丹心借一枝。

他日素车东浙路，怒涛岂必属鸱夷。

◆
◆
◆
◆

赏：张煌言，号苍水，南明抗清名将。1664 年抗清失败后被俘，同年被押往杭州，这首诗为临行前所作，语调悲怆。张苍水自知复明无望，国破家亡之际，抱必死之心，只希望能长眠于岳飞和于谦旁，并借伍子胥死后化为钱塘怒涛的典故，表明心志。全诗慷慨悲壮，令人扼腕。

57. Leaving My Hometown in August

By Zhang Huangyan（1620－1664 Ming Dynasty）

Where to? My country vanquished, home lost

My iconic heroes resting by West Lake.

The sun and moon shine over Yu's tomb;

Yue Fei's Temple still guards half the unconquered land.

I cannot compare with these two heroes

But given my loyalty I hope to rest by their sides.

White mourning carriages will one day crowd this road

In angry rolling tides like Wu Yun's I persist.

◆
◆
◆
◆

Notes:

1. Zhang Huangyan, also known as Zhang Cangshui, was a high ranking Ming Dynasty official. As a Ming loyalist, he led a resistance against the Qing army. Captured on a coastal island, he was escorted to Hangzhou (known then as Wulin) in August 1664. He wrote this poem before his escorted departure, well aware of his fate. He referred to the two heroes (Yu and Yue) buried by the West Lake, expressing his wish to be buried there as well. You can find his tomb by the West Lake.

2. Wu Zixu was a general and politician (circa 559-484 BC) and later became a role model for loyalty in Chinese culture. Legend has it that he became "the god of waves" after his unjust death and sought revenge in the form of angry rolling tidal bores in the Qiantang River.

58．过杭州故宫二首

〔南宋〕谢翱

其一

禾黍何人为守阍，落花台殿暗销魂。

朝元阁下归来燕，不见前头鹦鹉言。

其二

紫云楼阁宴流霞，今日凄凉佛子家。

残照下山花雾散，万年枝上挂袈裟。

◆
◆
◆
◆

赏：宋末元初爱国诗人谢翱以南宋遗民身份凭吊杭州故宫废址，抒发亡国之恨、故国之思。第一首写旧时宫室宗庙衰颓破毁、麦秀渐渐禾黍油油、"不见人归见燕归"的荒凉寂寥。第二首写旧时皇室宫殿已成菩萨的庙宇，昔日繁华不再，故国不堪回首。该诗含蓄指责叹惋南宋君臣贪图眼豫、苟且偷安以至亡国的悲剧。

58. Passing the Former Palace in Hangzhou

By Xie Ao (1249—1295 Southern Song Dynasty)

Grass grows wild, not a soul guards the palace ruins;

Fading blooms by the old court hall bring sorrow.

Swallows still return to Chaoyuan Pavilion;

Yet no trace of the loquacious parrot from years past.

Purple Cloud Pavilion once flowed with wine and colorful clouds;

Now a desolate dwelling for wandering monks.

Sunset's glow dissipates mist, shrouding foliage below;

Monks' kasayas drape the holly bushes.

◆
◆
◆
◆

Note: Hangzhou, was the capital of the Southern Song

Dynasty from 1138 to 1276. The poet Xie described the desolate scene of the former Southern Song Dynasty palace after the fall of Hangzhou. It became a dwelling place for the wandering monks who came from the north.

59．酬洪昇

〔清〕朱彝尊

金台酒坐劈红笺，云散星离又十年。

海内诗家洪玉父，禁中乐府柳屯田。

梧桐夜雨词凄绝，苡薏明珠谤偶然。

白发相逢岂容易，津头且揽下河船。

◆
◆
◆
◆

赏：朱彝尊的诗多笔力雅健、事典赡博。这首是朱彝尊在杭州小住并与洪昇相遇时而作的酬唱诗，以回忆当年京城雅会分笺赋诗的欢情落笔，叙写与剧作家洪昇的友情。朱氏赞其才华如洪炎、柳永。"苡薏明珠"代指遭人诬谤，诗人为好友被弹劾入狱的遭遇感到愤慨，对文网高张的政治进行了含蓄批判。此诗是其"醇雅"诗论的体现，婉而多讽，怨而不怒，典雅深蕴。

59. Entertaining Hong Sheng

By Zhu Yizun(1629—1709 Qing Dynasty)

Drinking in the capital, inscribing poems on red paper

Like drifting clouds, we have not seen each other in ten years.

You are now the country's venerated poet Hong

Equal in fame as the court lyricist Liu.

"Parasol trees in the evening drizzle, " beautifully touching

Opponents slain in vain, mistaking pearl for barley.

It is not likely we will meet again as old men;

Let's board a boat at the dock and float afar.

❖
❖
❖
❖

Note: Hong Sheng was a renowned playwright in the Qing

Dynasty. "The Palace of Eternal Youth" is his well-known masterpiece.

60. 木兰花慢·武林归舟中作

〔清〕董士锡

看斜阳一缕，刚送得，片帆归。 正岸绕孤城，波回野渡，月暗闲堤。 依稀是谁相忆？ 但轻魂、如梦逐烟飞。 赢得双双泪眼，从教浣尽罗衣。

江南几日又天涯，谁与寄相思？ 怅夜夜霜花，空林开遍，也只侬知。 安排十分秋色，便芳菲、总是别离时。 惟有醉将醹醁，任他柔橹轻移。

◆
◆
◆
◆

赏：自古诗词多写离情，"相见时难别亦难"是最经典的名句。这首离情词以归舟为中心意象，双双泪眼，几日又天涯，小聚又分别，全诗一波三折，跌宕起伏，离情幽怨至极。武林即杭州，此词的副词和连词如"正""但""又""只""惟"等，写出了相聚的短暂仓促，凄凉无限。但结尾甚妙，任柔橹轻移，依然美酒相送，道尽了聚少离多的恋人之间的无奈与深情。董士锡的词敛气循声、兴象风神，骚雅古怀。

60. Slow Tune of Magnolia—On a Boat Returning to Wulin

By Dong Shixi(1782—1831 Qing Dynasty)

A ray of the setting sun

Bids farewell to departing boats;

Welcomes homing sails.

The shoreline circles a lonely city;

Ripples retreat to the deserted dock;

The dim moon hangs over an empty embankment.

Who arises in vague memory?

Chasing vanishing mists in my dreams.

All has dissipated but for tears welling in my eyes

Dampening my clothes.

Setting off again after time in Jiangnan

To whom shall I reveal my yearning?

Disconsolate over night's frosted petals

Fallen over deserted woods

A scene only you know.

Nature exhibits full foliage

Admired at the time of separation.

I indulge in savory wine;

Let the gentle oar drift me farther.

❖
❖
❖
❖

Note: As an important member of the Changzhou Ci poetry school, Dong Shixi greatly influenced the development of Ci in the late Qing Dynasty. This is a perfect example of how Dong Shixi could bring the connotations of parting sorrows to a new level.

61. 晨出艮山门看秋景访徐艮生貌才

〔清〕项益寿

扁舟一棹入溪湾，隔岸红蓼隐白鹇。

选胜竭当图画里，招凉难得水云间。

清思惯寄三分竹，晓景贪看两面山。

黄叶树中徐稚完，闲可口许叩柴关。

◆
◆
◆
◆

　　赏：艮山门原为杭州古城东北门，南宋年间因汴京有艮岳，故改此门为艮山门，有不忘古都之意。艮山门在京杭大运河边，如今的运河上驳船日夜穿梭，周边商厦林立，热闹非凡。项益寿在诗中记录了当时秋日艮山门周边的种种景致，溪湾扁舟、红蓼白鹇、远山翠竹，沿这样一幅宁静恬淡的诗画长卷去探望老友，令人羡慕。

61. Leaving Genshan Gate at Dawn for an Autumn Outing and Visiting Xu on the Way

By Xiang Yishou（Qing Dynasty）

Propelling a canoe through the winding brook.

White pheasants hide among red knotweed on the opposite shore.

Such scenic spots exist only on canvas.

Most refreshing is where water and clouds merge.

For poetic inspiration, turn to bamboo groves.

For scenery indulgence, marvel the mountains along the river.

Xu Zhiwan resides among yellow-leaved trees

knocking on his thatched gate at my leisure, a pleasure.

◆
◆
◆
◆

Note: Now a bustling canal park with incessant canal transportation, lush trees and shrubs, the Genshan Gate used to be one of the city gates of ancient Hangzhou. This poem paints a tranquil picture of what the Genshan Gate looked like in the Qing Dynasty.

62. 西湖竹枝词二首

〔清〕陈璨

其一

清明土步鱼初美，重九团脐蟹正肥。

莫怪白公抛不得，便论食品亦忘归。

其二

王坟蚕豆鹦哥绿，龙井杨梅鹤顶丹。

更采湖莼如雉尾，尝新四月劝加餐。

◆
◆
◆
◆

赏：竹枝词原是流传于沅湘、巴渝一带的民歌，文人借用传统"竹枝"体创作诗句，受到欢迎。

其一，此诗清新、通俗，以不同时节的食物反映了民间质朴的生活情趣。土步鱼以清明前出网为佳。"杭州以土步鱼为上品"，肉质松嫩。清明时节，土步鱼美味；重阳节的雌蟹正肥美。难怪白居易不愿离开杭州，美味的食物也会让人流连忘返。

其二，西湖地道风物入诗。《西湖新志》记载：南屏山邵皇亲坟左侧有地产蚕豆，颗大而味鲜，杭人呼为"王坟豆"。此诗运用比喻，形象地将蚕豆比作鹦鹉的羽毛。龙井的杨梅红得像丹顶鹤的冠。《齐民要术》有言："四月莼生，茎而未叶，名作雉尾莼，第一肥美。"诗人深得传统精髓，"不时，不食"，那么不妨用这些春季鲜物给自己加个餐吧。

62. West Lake Bamboo Songs

By Chen Can (Qing Dynasty)

Mudskippers during Tomb Sweeping are delicious,

Female crabs at Double Ninth the most exquisite.

No wonder poet Bai resisted leaving Hangzhou;

Its savory cuisine seduces.

The local broad beans are green as a parrot's feather;

The bayberries at Dragon Well, red as a Japanese crane's crown.

The lake's water shields like pheasants' tails;

To savor in April, cook more white rice.

❖
❖
❖
❖

Note: Bamboo songs are verses similar to ballads. The

poet Yang Weizhen of the Yuan Dynasty first wrote about the West Lake in this folk ballad style. Poem No.33 was one of his earliest.

63．东郊土物藕粉

〔清〕姚思勤

谁碾玉玲珑，绕磨滴芳液。

攫泥本不染，渍粉讵太白。

铺夌暴秋阳，片片银刀画。

一撮点汤调，犀匙溜滑泽。

◈
◈
◈
◈

赏：《杭州府志》有云："春藕汁去浑晒粉，西湖所出为良。"诗人诗意地描绘了藕出淤泥而不染，以及碾磨、暴晒、削片、冲泡的过程。从诗中"片片银刀画"中可看出，当时的西湖藕粉是手工削出的小薄片状，而非常见的颗粒状。在诗人看来，风景宜入诗、风物亦可入诗，别有风味。

63. A Lake East Delicacy: Lotus Root Starch

By Yao Siqin (Qing Dynasty)

Who is grinding delicate jade?

Fragrant juice dripping off the millstone.

Pulled from deep mud, clean and pure

Their starch white as snow.

Dried on a bamboo flat under the blazing sun;

Sliced thin with a shining knife.

Fetch some to make thick porridge

Dripping like honey from a rhino horn spoon.

Note：In late fall，lotus roots are harvested from deep in mud. They can be enjoyed in many ways. Its starch，for example，can be used as a savory desert topped with osmanthus flavored sugar.

64．江涨桥步月

〔清〕张洵

北郭月初上，江桥策杖还。

天空秋影澹，风定市声闲。

隐隐渔家火，遥遥湖上山。

沿缘独归去，门巷未曾关。

◆
◆
◆
◆

赏：江涨桥位于今杭州市拱墅区，因古代海潮直逼此地而得名，不远处有潮王庙，为纪念一位筑德胜坝挡潮而鞠躬尽瘁的古人而建。桥东北有香积寺，东南有富义仓。江涨桥古为三孔石拱桥，雄伟壮观，是运河出入杭城的关口。此桥在古诗文中常用来代指杭州，如苏东坡的"还将梦魂去，一夜到江涨"。诗人张洵于秋日的一个傍晚策杖从江涨桥回返，月上北郭、秋空宁静、风定市闲，远处点点渔火。西湖边青山隐约，一派祥和之象。

64. Strolling River Crest Bridge under Moonlight

By Zhang Xun (Qing Dynasty)

The moon rises over the northern city;

I stroll from the bridge with my cane.

The autumn sky is tranquil;

In abated wind the market quiets.

Faint fishing lights dim and flickering

Lakeside mountains rise in the distance.

Walking the path alone

Gates and courtyards are flung wide open.

◆

◆

◆

◆

Note: The River Crest Bridge was once the main gate on

the Grand Canal leading in and out of Hangzhou. Ocean tides once reached as far as this gate，hence the name River Crest Bridge.

65．拱宸桥夕发

〔清〕宋伯鲁

树映陂塘雪映帘，三年留滞岂终淹。

故人已似沉沉伙，好句争传昔昔盐。

流水马声双槛外，夕阳塔影两山尖。

归期未筮翻西去，愁绝河桥翠柳纤。

❖
❖
❖
❖

赏：拱宸桥是京杭大运河南端的标志。"宸"指帝王所居之处，"拱"即拱手相迎之意，故拱宸桥象征着对古代帝王南巡杭州时的相迎与敬意。清末维新派宋伯鲁积极参与"百日维新"，变法失败后，遭革职通缉。此诗为其避祸途中，落脚杭州时所作。冬日雪后的傍晚，诗人宋伯鲁登船从杭州的拱宸桥出发，故人云散星离，自己前途叵测，诗句充满萧瑟凄凉之感。

65. Setting off at Dusk from Gongchen Bridge

By Song Bolu（Qing Dynasty）

Trees reflected in the river, snow on the banks

Three years of exile will not discourage my heart.

Though all acquaintances seem to have disappeared

I recall when we responded to others' great poems.

Flowing water and horses' hooves pass double fences;

The setting sun casts a pagoda's shadow between two peaks.

Poised to venture west with no set return

The delicate green willows and bridge share my sorrow.

◆
◆
◆
◆

Note: The poet was associated with reform-minded consultants of Emperor Guangxu in 1898. The Wuxu Reform lasted only a little over a hundred days due to strong oppositions from Empress Dowager Cixi. Some of the reformers were captured and executed, and some went into hiding or fled abroad. The poet wrote this poem while in exile.

66．黄金缕

〔北宋〕司马槱

妾本钱塘江上住。 花落花开，不管流年度。 燕子衔将春色去，纱窗几阵黄梅雨。

斜插犀梳云半吐，檀板轻敲，唱彻黄金缕。 望断行云无觅处，梦回明月生南浦。

◆
◆
◆
◆

赏：宋代临安（杭州）是与南京齐名的商业都市，也是著名的繁华之地。钱塘江一带犹如秦淮河边，歌楼妓馆比肩而立，箫管丝竹悠扬不绝。此词上片假拟歌女苏小小托梦自我倾诉，如怨如诉。下片写诗人梦醒之后回忆钱塘歌女的容貌举止与心迹，最后发出佳人无处可觅，唯明月伴我梦回南浦的感慨。诗词贵朦胧，此词可贵之处在于意蕴丰富却又不晦涩玄奥。

66. To the Tune of the Gold-Threaded Couture

By Sima You (Northern Song Dynasty)

I, a humble woman, resides by Qiantang River.

Flowers fade and bloom;

My youth slips idly by.

Swallows pack up spring colors and fly away;

A fine rain mists the window screen.

A rhino comb atilt in your hair like a crescent moon in dark clouds;

Wood clappers beat in unison;

The melody of the Gold-Threaded Couture is sung.

Under drifting clouds, you are nowhere to be found;

In my dream, the bright moon rises over the south bank.

◆
◆
◆
◆

Note：The poet Sima You died in Hangzhou as a governor during the Song Dynasty. It was said that he had a dream one night，in which the legendary beautiful courtesan Su Xiaoxiao recited the first stanza in the poem above to him. Sima You woke up and wrote the second stanza in response. Su the courtesan was the subject of many poems and lyrics. Poems No. 72 and No. 79 also reference her.

67．咏柳

〔唐〕贺知章

碧玉妆成一树高，万条垂下绿丝绦。

不知细叶谁裁出，二月春风似剪刀。

◆
◆
◆
◆

赏：唐朝诗人贺知章是浙江历史上首位有详细记载的状元，出生于今杭州萧山蜀山街道。贺诗大多朴素清新、不事雕琢，如"少小离家""鬓衰而归"，虽似乡野之语，却于平淡处见自然。自古咏柳之句数不胜数，或绮丽或事典，曲尽其妙，后人很难超越。贺知章则以奇思妙想，用一把寻常"剪刀"轻巧剪出千古名句，令人叫绝。

67. Ode to Willows

By He Zhizhang (circa 659−744 Tang Dynasty)

Green jade adorns the majestic willow tree;

Thousands of emerald silk ribbons dangle with grace.

Who tailors its leaves into such fine shape?

Spring breezes in the second lunar moon work like scissors.

◆

◆

◆

◆

Note: The poet He Zhizhang is well-known for his creative but easy to understand poems. While most of his contemporaries used allusions after allusions to flaunt their knowledge, He Zhizhang refused such practice. He retired to his hometown at the age of 85 (after five decades of service in the court).

68. 清平乐·夏日游湖

〔南宋〕朱淑真

恼烟撩露，留我须臾住。 携手藕花湖上路，一霎黄梅细雨。

娇痴不怕人猜，和衣睡倒人怀。 最是分携时候，归来懒傍妆台。

◆
◆
◆
◆

赏：钱塘人朱淑真是唐宋以来留存作品最丰富的女词人之一，其词作多率性热烈。这是一篇叙事言情之词，记叙一次与恋人携手游西湖的经历，刻画了一个感情异常率真、愉快的少女形象。黄梅细雨，藕花湖边，格外朦胧优美。词的下片写躲雨时的心态。"娇痴不怕人猜，和衣睡倒人怀"的女子形象在宋词里别具一格，大胆开朗。分手回家也懒得照镜梳妆，千情百态，描绘细致，人物形象栩栩如生。

68. To the Tune of the Qing-Ping Songs of Yuefu—

Along a Lake in Summer

By Zhu Shuzhen（1135—1180 Southern Song Dynasty）

Misty fog traps dew;

Keeps me lingering.

Hand in hand, we stroll along a lake full of lotus blossoms;

Plum season's fine rain suddenly descends.

Tender affections, oblivious to curious onlookers;

I bury myself in your chest.

Leaving you is always hardest;

I stand idly by the dressing table after my return.

◆

◆

◆

◆

Note：The poetess Zhu Shuzhen was renowned for her beautiful poems and lyrics. Some scholars think poem No. 55 also was written by her.

69. 浣溪沙·清明

〔南宋〕朱淑真

春巷夭桃吐绛英，春衣初试薄罗轻。 风和烟暖燕巢成。
小院湘帘闲不卷，曲房朱户闷长扃。 恼人光景又清明。

◆
◆
◆
◆

赏：朱淑真词，风致之佳，词情之妙，不亚于李易安。宋代闺秀，淑真、易安并称"隽才"。此词便是一首风致极佳、词情极妙的闺怨词，也是伤春惜时之词。杭州西湖的春天桃花灼灼，罗衣初成，归来的燕子筑巢屋檐下。然庭院深幽，湘帘不卷，深闺中人的惆怅、落寞跃然纸上，与开篇的热闹和华丽形成强烈的对比。

69. To the Tune of Silk Rinsing Stream—Qingming

By Zhu Shuzhen (1135—1180 Southern Song Dynasty)

In the alley, spring peach blooms unfurl in scarlet;

I don my delicate spring silk garments.

Swallows build their nests amid gentle breezes and warm mist.

Mottled bamboo curtains drape low in the courtyard;

The vermilion gate shut tight, my boudoir is stifling.

The unwelcome Qingming season will soon return.

◆
◆
◆
◆

Note: To learn more about the poetess, please refer to

poem No. 68. Many of her poems and lyrics are about love

sorrow and heartbreaking partings. Qingming signals the end of spring. In a Confucian society，girls were not allowed to venture out of their courtyards too often before getting married.

70．与颜钱塘登樟亭望潮作

〔唐〕孟浩然

百里闻雷震，鸣弦暂辍弹。

府中连骑出，江上待潮观。

照日秋云迥，浮天渤澥宽。

惊涛来似雪，一坐凛生寒。

◆
◆
◆
◆

赏：中国的诗歌类别中，除常见的伤春、悲秋、闺怨、别离等，还有一个非常独特的题材——观潮。钱塘江大潮举世无双，自古以来无数诗人在江边留下了数不胜数的观潮诗，甚至连日本僧人也不例外，感慨大潮"雪作山耶云作花，崔嵬白浪及天涯"。诗人在首联中先营造出一种紧张的气氛——百里之外便隐约闻雷鸣，知府大人停止了弹琴，众人随后快马而出来江边观潮。诗人用了巨浪滔天、惊涛似雪两个比喻，并以江潮带来的阵阵寒意收尾，感受细腻，在众多观潮诗中别具一格。

70. Ascending Zhang Tower to View the Tidal Bore with Yan the Prefect of Qiantang

By Meng Haoran (689−740 Tang Dynasty)

Thunder reverberates over one hundred li;

The prefect stops plucking his string instrument.

One by one people ride their horses out of the prefect's hall

Flocking riverside to view the tidal bore.

The sun shines over high autumn clouds;

The vast ocean stretches to a distant skyline.

Mighty waves roll, crashing like an avalanche;

Spectators brace against chilly breezes.

◆
◆
◆
◆

Note：The Qiantang River's tidal bore is world famous for being the largest of its kind. On every lunar August 18th，the bore can reach up to 9 feet in height，and travel at up to 40 km per hour（25 miles an hour）. The poet wrote about this experience with his friend. Poem No. 50 also is a lyric about tidal bore viewing.

71. 忆杭州西湖

〔北宋〕范仲淹

长忆西湖胜鉴湖，春波千顷绿如铺。

吾皇不让明皇美，可赐疏狂贺老无。

◆
◆
◆
◆

　　赏：范仲淹主张诗歌创作要忠于生活现实，符合时事，不空言。这首诗以回忆西湖为题，却以论人论事为主。第一句直言西湖春波千顷胜过浙江绍兴的鉴湖。鉴湖为浙江名湖之一，有"鉴湖八百里"的壮阔之美。第二句转入论人论事，将宋仁宗与唐明皇相比，寄寓了明君惜才的期望。

71. West Lake of Hangzhou in Memory

By Fan Zhongyan（989－1052 Northern Song Dynasty）

In my memory, West Lake's glory surpasses Lake Jian's

A thousand acres of spring lake rippling, green as grass.

Your Majesty, as virtuous and wise as Emperor Ming

Could you bestow me the lake, like the lucky poet He?

◆
◆
◆
◆

Note: Lake Jian is a lake not far from Hangzhou. When the poet He Zhizhang（who wrote poem No. 67）retired from the court, the emperor gifted him Lake Jian for his extended royal service.

72. 钱塘苏小歌

〔南朝〕无名氏

妾乘油壁车，郎骑青骢马。

何处结同心？西陵松柏下。

◆
◆
◆
◆

赏：杭州苏小小的名字最早见于南朝陈徐陵所编《玉台新咏》卷十的《钱塘苏小歌》。此诗以"妾"的口吻讲述了自己与"郎"相约定情西湖孤山的故事，描绘了一乘一骑、一车一马，郎情妾意，自由奔放。唐朝后小小的形象转变为歌妓。苏小小逐渐成为许多诗歌、词曲的对象。

72. The Song of Su Xiao of Qiantang

By Anonymous(Southern Song Dynasty)

I ride in a lacquered carriage

You on a piebald horse.

Where to tie our love knot?

Under Xiling's pine cypresses.

◆

◆

◆

◆

Note: Su appears in many poems and lyrics, as in No. 66

and No. 79.

73. 雪后从西兴晚渡钱塘江

〔清〕查慎行

牛车没毂水沙浑，暗长春潮二尺痕。

万灶铺烟沉海戍，两山衔雪束江壖。

船开渡口愁将晚，月到圆时过上元。

莫负承平好风景，河塘灯火闹黄昏。

❖
❖
❖
❖

赏：诗人查慎行为清初六家之一，当时东南诗坛的领袖；他也是小说家金庸的先祖，《鹿鼎记》中的回目都是集查慎行诗中的对句而成。查慎行诗风清新隽永，白描中屡有妙词迭出，如末联"河塘灯火闹黄昏"中的"闹"字，顿使对岸晦暗的灯火鲜活明亮起来，让人过目不忘。西兴渡古为固陵渡、西陵渡，吴越时人们认为"陵"字不吉，遂改为西兴。西兴渡历为重要渡口，也是当年浙东唐诗之路的打卡之地，杜甫就曾到过西陵渡，留有诗作一首。

73. Crossing Qiantang River from Xixing Ferry after Snow

By Zha Shenxing (1650—1727 Qing Dynasty)

Muddy river rises above the wheels of my oxen cart;

An undetected spring tide surges two feet high.

Smoke from ten thousand chimneys blankets the river mouth;

Snow-covered twin mountains flank mighty torrents.

The delayed boat departs the ferry at dusk;

When the full moon rises, the Lantern Festival will begin.

Cherish this beautiful scene of peace and prosperity;

Twinkling lights celebrate dusk along the riverbank.

◆
◆
◆
◆

Note: A notable member of the scholarly Zha clan of

Haining, the poet was a well-known figure amongst the Qing Dynasty literati. Jin Yong (from the same Zha clan) used many of the poet's lines as chapter titles for some of his popular martial arts novels such as *The Legend of the Condor Heroes*.

74. 题西湖僧舍壁

〔北宋〕清顺

竹暗不通日，泉声落如雨。

春风自有期，桃李乱深坞。

◆
◆
◆
◆

赏：题壁诗始于两汉，盛于唐宋。《竹坡诗话》中载："东坡游西湖，于僧舍壁间见小诗，问谁所作，或告以钱塘僧清顺，即日求得之，一见甚喜，而顺之名出矣。"清顺为西湖北山垂云庵僧，与苏轼同时，著名诗僧。此诗古朴凝练，蕴含禅意。首句以竹映蔽日光营造幽静之感。第二句表达了一种"动"的意趣，动静结合，愈显幽静深远。春风有期，桃花开落，自然而然。

74. Inscribed on a Wall of a Monks' Dormitory by West Lake

By Qing Shun (Northern Song Dynasty)

Thick bamboo groves block the sunshine;

A cascading stream showers like rain.

Spring breezes arrive on their own;

Peach plum blossoms riot in a deep ravine.

◆
◆
◆
◆

Note: It has been a Chinese tradition to inscribe poems on suitable surfaces such as walls, columns and cliff sides etc. Many great poems were recorded in that way. This poem, by a monk named Qing Shun, was inscribed on the wall of a monks' dorm by the West Lake. Su the great poet enjoyed visiting temples and monasteries around the West Lake when serving as governor of Hangzhou. He admired this poem and befriended the monk poet. The two exchanged several poems according to "Zhupo's notes on poets and poetry."

75. 晚宿江涨桥

〔北宋〕李新

鸟径青山外，人家苦竹边。

江城悬夜锁，鱼市散空船。

岸静涵秋月，林昏宿水烟。

又寻僧榻卧，夜冷欲无眠。

❖
❖
❖
❖

赏：沿运河杭州段诗路寻踪，免不了提到这首诗。从前经由运河进出杭州，江涨桥是其中一进出口，地位特殊，也代指杭州，如苏轼的"还将梦魂去，一夜到江涨"所言。那时晚上会关闭城门，夜宿江涨也就不足为奇了。白天的喧嚣散尽，卖鱼桥鱼市空船四散。宁静的河岸滋养着秋月，朦胧的树林在雾蒙蒙的水边歇息，孤寂清冷之感颇有古拱墅八景之一"江涨暮雨"的韵味。

75. Lodging by River Crest Bridge

By Li Xin(1062—? Northern Song Dynasty)

Birds fly beyond the green mountains;

Residents reside near bitter bamboo groves.

A night lock shutters the river gate;

At the fish market's close, empty boats scatter.

The serene riverbank nourishes the autumn moon;

Dusky woods rest by misty water.

In a temple I seek a monk's futon;

The cold keeps me awake all night.

◆
◆
◆
◆

Note: Please refer to poem No. 64 for an explanation about River Crest Bridge.

76. 南屏晚钟

〔明〕王洧

涑水崖碑半绿苔，春游谁向此山来。

晚烟深处蒲牢响，僧自城中应供回。

◆
◆
◆
◆

赏：西湖边的南屏山因"形若象卷，状若屏开"而得名。吴越王在南屏山开启了以惠日永明寺为主体的佛国山的修建，宋太宗更寺名为寿宁禅寺，宋高宗最后更名为如今的净慈寺。儒家历来有"钟鼓道志"的传统，后受佛教影响，"晨钟"也慢慢演变为"晚钟""晚钟""暮钟"及"夜半钟声到客船"中的"半夜钟"。"烟寺晚钟"这一"潇湘八景"之一的经典意象在文人士大夫心中得以确立。而王洧的"烟晚深处蒲牢（钟声）响"也从另一侧面佐证了这一漫长的演变过程。末句表明因当时净慈寺在城外，夜晚城门关闭，南屏的钟声便是在提醒城中化缘的僧侣们该回寺院了。

76. Evening Bell Tolls at Nanping Hill

By Wang Wei (Ming Dynasty)

Green moss conceals half the inscribed cliff;

In spring, who ventures to this mountain?

At dusk, a bell tolls deep in the misty woods

Calling back the mendicant monks in the city.

◆

◆

◆

◆

Note: Nanping Hill is one of West Lake's ten scenic spots. Formerly, the bell (housed at the Jinci Temple) was outside the city gate. When it tolled at dusk, the mendicant monks wandering inside the city gate knew it was time to return or the gate would lock them out.

77. 南屏晚钟

〔清〕弘历

湖山四面画为屏，合有钟声警众声。

唐宋至今诸物改，霜天惟此未曾更。

❖
◆
◆
◆
❖

赏：清乾隆皇帝六下江南，每次到西湖都要留下御笔和诗作，
这首《南屏晚钟》便是其中之一。自王洧的《南屏晚钟》之后，南屏
晚钟便出现在数不清的诗人笔下，乾隆没有在辞藻上多下功夫，
而是另辟蹊径，在钟声的警世意义上做文章。自唐宋以来大千世
界早已物是人非，唯霜天如一亘古不变。这一有限与无限，刹那
和永恒之间的终极烦恼，恰似元朝诗人方回"万古一丸拿不去，夜
深朗月浸澄湖"的感慨一样，引发共鸣。

77. Evening Bell Tolls at Nanping Hill

By Hong Li (1711—1799 Qing Dynasty)

The lake and surrounding mountains, like paintings on canvas,

Resounding bells awaken every mortal being.

All has changed since the Tang and Song dynasties;

The autumn sky remains unchanged.

◆
◆
◆
◆

Note: Please refer to poem No. 76 for more information about Nanping Hill. Emperor Qianlong made six trips to Hangzhou in his life. He inscribed many poems around the West Lake. This poem is one of them.

78．西湖春日

〔北宋〕王安国

争得才如杜牧之，试来湖上辄题诗。

春烟寺院敲茶鼓，夕照楼台卓酒旗。

浓吐杂芳熏嶽崿，湿飞双翠破涟漪。

人间幸有蓑兼笠，且上渔舟作钓师。

◆
◆
◆
◆

赏：杜牧才华超卓，游历山水后挥笔题咏留下了许多名作。诗人开篇以感喟企慕的语气，显露对西湖的赞美之情。第二、三句描摹了西湖春景：春烟寺院、山岩春花吐芳、湖边楼台亭榭、湖中画船穿梭，一派旖旎风光。最后一句呼应首句，表达了留恋杭州、栖身湖山的雅志。此外，诗人王安国是宰相王安石的弟弟，器识磊落。

78. A Spring Day on West Lake

By Wang Anguo（1028—1074 Northern Song Dynasty）

I wish to be as talented as the great Poet Du Mu

Who composes with ease afloat on a lake.

A temple cloaked in spring mist beats its tea drum;

A tavern's wine pennant flutters in the glowing sunset.

Wild blossoms perfume the surrounding peaks;

A pair of painted boats disturb the water's ripples.

Fortunate to have palm-bark capes and bamboo hats

For now, I board a fish junk to angle.

◆
◆
◆
◆

Note：Wang Anguo was the younger brother of Wang

Anshi. The image of "an angler" in classic Chinese is usually associated with talented scholars who were bored with officialdom and politics and chose to seek peace and enjoyment in nature instead.

79．苏小小歌

〔唐〕温庭筠

买莲莫破券，买酒莫解金。

酒里春容抱离恨，水中莲子怀芳心。

吴宫女儿腰似束，家在钱唐小江曲。

一自檀郎逐便风，门前春水年年绿。

◆
◆
◆
◆

赏：此诗借乐府古题，以杭州苏小小之名，写良人离去，年华不再。此诗场景鲜活：一位佳人举杯消愁，思念情郎，正如柳永所说"衣带渐宽终不悔，为伊消得人憔悴"。酒中映出的脸，是离别的哀愁。水中莲子带有女子的情怀。情郎坐船乘风而去，从此杳无音信。门外西湖春水碧绿一如既往，年年岁岁。此诗轻巧艳丽又不失清新温婉，不愧为温庭筠这位花间鼻祖的名作！

79. The Song of Su Xiaoxiao

By Wen Tingyun (circa 801—866 Tang Dynasty)

Buy not affection with gold

Nor wine to sooth your heart.

The face reflected in my wine expresses parting grief;

Lotus seeds in water nurture tender hearts.

My waist slender from sorrow

By the meandering tributary of Qiantang I reside.

My lover boarded a boat in full sail, never heard from again;

Beyond my door, spring water green as always, year after year.

❖
❖
❖
❖

Note: Su the courtesan was the subject of many poems and lyrics. Both No. 66 and No. 72 are related to her as well.

80. 应举题钱塘公馆内

〔唐〕周匡物

万里茫茫天堑遥，秦皇底事不安桥。

钱塘江口无钱过，又阻西陵两信潮。

◆
◆
◆
◆

赏：从前举子赶考，但凡家贫的，都只能徒步应举，所谓"落魄风尘，怀刺不偶"，周匡物便是一例。周匡物为漳州人，于唐元和年间进士及第，在诗坛颇有盛名，但当年赶考途中却颇为狼狈。他因无钱坐渡船过江，小船又经不起钱塘江的大潮汛，只得望江兴叹，题此诗于钱塘公馆内。后被郡守得知，怪罪津吏，自此天下渡船皆不敢收举子钱，遂成佳话。

80. Inscribing Qiantang Lodge

By Zhou Kuangwu (Tang Dynasty)

My destination distant, a mighty river looms ahead;

Why didn't the Qin Emperor build a bridge here?

I have no money for the ferry and

The impassable tidal bore surges by Xinling twice daily.

◆
◆
◆
◆

Note: The Poet Zhou was from a poor family. He walked his way to the capital for the imperial examination. With no money to pay for the ferry, he was unable to cross the Qiantang River. He inscribed this poem on the wall at his lodging in lament. A passing prefect later read the poem, and then reprimanded the ferry official. From then on，no ferry clerk dared to ask imperial examinees for ferry fare.

81. 观潮

〔日本〕策彦周良

雪作山耶云作花，崔嵬白浪及天涯。

势风沙矣声雷震，肠断钱塘十万家。

◆
◆
◆
◆

赏：策彦周良为日本临济宗高僧，汉文功底深厚，工于诗，曾于1539 年和 1547 年两度作为遣明副使和正使率团来中国。他和嘉靖朝文人多有唱和，人称"读其文，有班马之余风也；诵其诗，有二唐之遗响也"，嘉靖帝赐诗"奇哉才业与渊深，佳作一章波澜心"。他访问杭州期间恰逢八月十八大潮，因从小仰慕苏轼咏潮诗中的"八月十八潮，壮观天下无"，于观潮后特和此诗。诗中对钱江大潮的声、色、形、势进行了精准描绘，以雪山云花为形色，天涯白浪为势，风沙雷震为声，以肠断钱塘十万人家的夸张手法描摹大潮的壮观恢宏。此为观潮诗之佳作，也是文明互赏互鉴的典范。

81. Viewing the Tidal Bore

By Ceyan Zhouliang（Japanese，1501—1579）

Mountains of snow, clouds of blossoms,

Colossal white waves descend from the skyline.

Like a mighty sandstorm roaring thunderously

Frightening Qiantang's ten thousand households.

◆
◆
◆
◆

Note: After the Han and Tang Dynasties, the Ming Dynasty was another high point in China's diplomatic relationships with other countries. While Zheng He's mighty fleet visited India, Arabia and even Africa, many foreigners came to visit and study in China. Ceyan Zhouliang（Sakugen

Shūryō) was one of them，forging friendly relations with many Chinese poets，even the Chinese emperor himself. This poem describes his tidal bore viewing experience in Hangzhou.

82. 送惠思归钱塘

〔北宋〕司马光

孤岫平湖外，禅房老柏阴。

倦游谙浊世，独往遂初心。

夜雨灯窗迥，秋苔屐齿深。

勿锄山径草，便有俗人寻。

◆
◆
◆
◆
◆

　　赏：惠思是孤山高僧，余杭人，与梅尧臣、苏轼、苏辙、司马光、王安石等人都有交谊。此诗先写西湖孤山上禅寺的外景，孤山平湖，古木森森。人世纷繁让人倦怠，而禅寺夜雨中灯火飘摇，秋苔幽深少有人迹。最后以劝诫的语气，表达了诗人心向佛老的超然心境，不用除掉山径野草，这样可能会招徕更多的喧扰。司马光推崇"文以载道",认为华而不实的诗无用,他称赏平淡闲远,抒发真性情的诗歌。

82. Sending Huisi to Qiantang

By Sima Guang（1019—1086 Northern Song Dynasty）

The Lonely Mountain stands by the calm lake；

A weathered cypress shades the meditation room.

Disillusioned by the tumultuous mundane world

My heart seeks a Buddhist path.

A light illuminates a window in the evening drizzle；

Clogs leave deep imprints in the autumn moss.

Do not hoe the weeds on the mountain path and

No one will disturb your hermitage.

❖
❖
❖
❖

Note：Sima Guang once served as premier in the Song Dynasty.

83. 清平乐·兰曰国香

〔南宋〕张炎

孤花一叶，比似前时别。 烟水茫茫无处说，冷却西湖残月。

贞芳只合深山，红尘了不相关。 留得许多清影，幽香不到人间。

◆
◆
◆
◆

赏：张炎为南宋初年名将张俊六世孙，正当而立之年，元兵攻破临安，祖父被杀，家产被抄，从此流落江南。诗人画家郑思肖（南翁）善画无根之兰，取江山易主、草木无处扎根之意，特画一幅孤花一叶的兰草图送给张炎。词人有感而发，对郑思肖隐而不仕的高尚情操深为钦佩。词中虽显亡国之痛，然词风清空苍凉，意境不俗。

83. To the Tune of Qing-Ping Songs of Yuefu—

To the Chinese Ground Orchid

By Zhang Yan（1248—1320 Southern Song Dynasty）

A lonely blossom with a single leaf

Much like the one I left behind.

The misty water is vast, no acquaintances are in sight;

The solitary crescent moon hangs over West Lake.

Such pure beauty belongs only deep in the mountains

An orchid without worldly attachments.

Casting numerous delicate shadows

Its faint fragrance is not for this world.

◆
◆
◆
◆

Note: The poet introduces this piece by reference to the Chinese ground orchid, a flower that is subtle of color and fragrance but endowed with what some regarded as heavenly purity. The poet wonders where he can see the orchid in his contemporary writings. He writes, "I am fortunate to see it in a few brush strokes by my friend Nan the Senior. This poem is to commemorate this joyful experience."

After Hangzhou fell, many Southern Song loyalists refused to cooperate. Nan the Senior was known for painting orchids with no roots to lament the fact that the country was in the hands of others, and that orchids now had no place to take root.

84．送客之杭

〔唐〕牟融

西风吹冷透貂裘，行色匆匆不暂留。

帆带夕阳投越浦，心随明月到杭州。

风清听漏惊乡梦，灯下闻歌乱别愁。

悬想到杭州兴地，尊前应与话离忧。

◆
◆
◆
◆

赏：关于此诗历来有争议，很多人认为不可能为牟融所作。能以一个成语和两句佳句流传后世的诗作并不多，《送客之杭》便是其一，其中的"行色匆匆"如今已为成语，"帆带夕阳投越浦，心随明月到杭州"更是为读者所熟悉。诗歌以刺骨西风起兴，联想到友人即将远行，不免惆怅。然而杭州自古为天下风流之地，故无需伤悲。虽风清听漏、灯下闻歌难免引起离愁，然而"出宿于干，饮饯于言"，以酒为友人践行，便是请求路神庇护友人旅途平安。这是朋友之间最朴素的祝福，情谊真切。

84. Sending a Guest to Hangzhou

By Mou Rong(？ －79 Han Dynasty)

Chilly westerly breezes penetrate my mink coat;

In hurried departure I won't detain you any longer.

A sail under the sunset's glow heads for the rivers of Yue;

The bright moon carries my heart to Hangzhou.

In gentle wind, a water clock interrupts my nostalgic dream

Listening to a melody by lamplight, parting sorrow arises.

Hangzhou is, after all, a prosperous prefect;

I bid you farewell over wine before your journey.

◆

◆

◆

◆

Note: This poem has been in circulation for hundreds of

years as penned by Mou Rong of the Tang Dynasty. More recent research reveals that Mou Rong who was a Han Dynasty official, couldn't have written this poem. Rather, it was most likely the work of an unknown Ming Dynasty poet who used Mou Rong's fame to get this in circulation, a common practice in ancient China.

85. 江城子·西湖感怀

〔南宋〕刘辰翁

涌金门外上船场，湖山堂，众贤堂。 到处凄凉，城角夜吹霜。 谁识两峰相对语，天惨惨，水茫茫。

月移疏影傍人墙，怕昏黄，又昏黄。 旧日朱门，四圣暗飘香。 驿使不来春又老，南共北，断人肠。

◆
◆
◆
◆

赏：刘辰翁为南宋末年著名爱国诗人。宋亡后，刘辰翁矢志不仕，回乡隐居而终。其词风兼容苏辛，因亡国之痛，豪放中带有沉郁和伤怀。此词开篇便连用三处西湖边地标而感慨"到几凄凉"，可谓"风景不殊，正自有山河之异"，手法与《忆秦娥》中的"烧灯节，朝京道上风和雪。风和雪，江山如旧，朝京人绝"如出一辙。

虽朱门依旧，四圣香飘，然河山已易主。末尾点出宋亡后社会秩序大乱，驿使迹绝，断人肝肠！

85. To the Tune of Jinling the River Town—Thoughts by West Lake

By Liu Chenweng（1232—1297 Southern Song to early Yuan Dynasty）

Boarding a boat outside the Yongjin Gate

Passing Mountain Lake Hall and

Sages Hall.

How melancholy!

A night horn resonating, frost descending on the city wall.

Two facing mountain peaks converse silently,

The sky above endless

The water below boundless.

Moonlight creeps through sparse shadows onto a wall,

Unwelcoming evenfall

At evenfall.

Memorial hall's vermilion gate stands as always;

The Four Sages' Shrine emanates faint aromas.

Spring fades, messenger couriers halted

From north to south

Unbearable sadness.

◆

◆

◆

◆

Note: This is a typical lyric about being psychologically displaced after the fall of the Southern Song. As a Song loyalist, the poet wrote of a scene still familiar but nevertheless melancholy, suffused with unbearable sadness.

86. 送别

李叔同

长亭外，古道边，芳草碧连天。晚风拂柳笛声残，夕阳山外山。

天之涯，地之角，知交半零落。一壶浊酒尽余欢，今宵别梦寒。

◆
◆
◆
◆

赏：《送别》是李叔同根据美国音乐家约翰·奥德威的《梦见家和母亲》(*Dreaming of Home and Mother*) 的旋律，以及日本音乐教育家犬童球溪所翻译的《旅愁》而改写的词。最早的译文如下：

西风起，秋渐深，秋容动客心。独身惆怅叹飘零，寒光照孤影。

忆故土，思故人，高堂会双亲。乡路迢迢何处寻，觉来梦断心。

　　后来，天涯五好友之一的诗人许幻园前来杭州和李话别，李叔同感慨万千，以长短句重新将此歌改为骊歌的形式表达对好友的离别之情。他的学生丰子恺所保留的手抄版就来源于此，其他添加部分无法证实是否为李叔同亲笔。"正当今夕断肠处，骊歌愁绝不忍听"，李叔同后更名为弘一法师，在杭州虎跑寺出家，当年所作《送别》感人至深，传唱至今。

86. Farewell

By Li Shutong (1880—1942)

Outside the rest pavilion, by the ancient pass

Endless green grass merges with the sky.

Evening breezes brush the willows, notes of a bamboo flute fade;

The sun sets over the mountain beyond.

From the edge of the sky to the rim of the earth

Acquaintances are few and far between.

One cup of cloudy wine enlightens the rest of the day;

No dreams of cold solitude tonight.

◆
◆
◆
◆

Note: Li Shutong, also known as Master Hongyi, was a master painter, educator, musician, dramatist, calligrapher, seal cutter, poet, as well as an ordained Buddhist monk in his later life. He wrote it to the melody of a mid-19th century song *Dreaming of Home and Mother* by American composer John P. Ordway. Li himself wrote only the first stanza; someone else added a second stanza after it became a well-known song in China under Li's name.

87. 虞美人·姑苏画莲

〔南宋〕韩淲

西湖十里孤山路。犹记荷花处。翠茎红蕊最关情。不是熏风、吹得晚来晴。

而今老去丹青底。醉腻娇相倚。棹歌声缓采香归。如梦如醒、新月照涟漪。

❖
❖
❖
❖

赏：这是一首回忆、怀念西湖美景的词。韩淲恬于荣利，雅志绝俗，清苦自持，一意以吟咏为事。词中上片先写西湖孤山，湖山相依，荷叶田田；夏日黄昏，云淡风轻，美景尤其令人难忘。下片写湖上采莲的欢快景象，悠扬的歌声里荡舟晚归，新月下西湖涟漪微漾。"犹记"和"而今"都点明了对西湖美景与美好往事的回忆与念想。

87. To the Tune of Beauty Yu—Painting Lotus Blossoms at Gusu

By Han Biao (1159—1224 Southern Song Dynasty)

Ten li on West Lake's winding pass to the Lonely Hill.

I still remember where lotus blossoms flourished.

Their tender green stalks and red stamens are most charming.

It is not a southerly breeze that

Scattered clouds at dusk.

Though the color on canvas has faded

Delicate blossoms still nestle affectionately among the leaves.

Background barcarolle while picking lotus flowers on the return.

As if in a dream, as if intoxicated

The crescent moon shines over the ripples on the lake.

◆
◆
◆
◆

Note：It is likely that the poet wrote this poem while admiring a painting of the West Lake lotus blossoms in Suzhou (Gusu). Although the painting has faded，the scene still evokes fond memories of the West Lake.

88．再和元礼春怀十首（其一）

〔北宋〕黄庭坚

回肠无奈别愁煎，待得鸾胶续断弦。

最忆钱塘风物苦，西湖月落采菱船。

◆
◆
◆
◆

赏：元礼是成都佳少年，在杭州浪荡多年，但才华横溢。后来有所收敛，但偶旧态复发。他与黄庭坚多有酬唱往来，此诗便是其一。诗中的"鸾胶再续"喻指好友重逢时相互酬唱，这里主要喻指两人的情感深厚、难分难舍。诗中也提到最怀念的还是曾经一起在西湖泛舟采菱的欢乐往事。

88. Responding to Yuanli's Poem about Spring (I)

By Huang Tingjian (1045—1105 Northern Song Dynasty)

Parting sorrow steeps at your departure;

I await our reunion over the next poetry exchange.

Most memorable are Qiantang's water chestnuts;

West Lake's moon descends on the fruit-gathering boat.

◆
◆
◆
◆

Note: Water chestnuts are tasty when in season. West Lake produces large quantities of these savory local delicacies.

89．忆钱塘

〔唐〕李廓

往岁东游鬓未凋，渡江曾驻木兰桡。

一千里色中秋月，十万军声半夜潮。

桂倚玉儿吟处雪，蓬遗苏丞舞时腰。

仍闻江上春来柳，依旧参差拂寺桥。

◆
◆
◆
◆

赏：诗人李廓为大唐宗室，27 岁进士及第，与姚合、贾岛等人多有唱和，时有佳句。该诗中"一千里色中秋月，十万军声半夜潮"为观潮名句；融融月色普照千里，夜半钱塘江潮汛犹如千军万马疾奔而来，极具感染力。将八月十五钱塘江潮汛之声喻为千军万马为李廓独创，流传甚广。《水浒传》中描写鲁智深圆寂一事可见作者有可能受李廓的影响。鲁智深在六和塔出家，半夜潮汛声来，将他从睡梦中惊醒。出于武夫的本能，他提起禅杖奔将出去欲与贼子拼命，得知为潮汛后，猛然想起五台山智真长老当年给他的偈语中有一句"听潮而圆，见信而寂"，方知彼时该圆寂，遂沐浴焚香结跏趺坐而终。

89. Qiantang in My Memory

By Li Kuo (? −851 Tang Dynasty)

I was still in my prime when traveling east;

At a river crossing I boarded a boat.

A thousand li of the mid-autumn moon full and bright,

A hundred thousand soldiers' battle cries echo in the mid-night tide.

Fragrant osmanthus trees delicate under moonlight;

Lotus blossoms twirl like young dancers of Su the Prefect.

I hear the spring willows by the river have sprouted

As always, their uneven tendrils brushing the temple bridge.

◆
◆
◆
◆

Note: Due to the unrivaled Qiantang River tidal bores,

tidal bore viewing has been a popular theme for poetry throughout the dynasties. In this poem, the poet applied his imaginations to the fullest by comparing the roaring sound to battle cries, which was noted and admired by generations of poets after him.

90．杭州故人信至齐安

〔北宋〕苏轼

昨夜风月清，梦到西湖上。

朝来闻好语，扣户得吴饷。

轻圆白晒荔，脆酽红螺酱。

更将西庵茶，劝我洗江瘴。

故人情义重，说我必西向。

一年两仆夫，千里问无恙。

相期结书社，未怕供诗帐。

还将梦魂去，一夜到江涨。

❖
❖
❖
❖

赏：苏轼因诗获罪，被贬谪去往黄州。隋朝始以齐安郡为黄州。杭州旧友王复、张弼、辩才、无择诸人不惧受牵连，写信问候，并寄送了吴馔美食白晒荔干、红螺酱、西庵茶等犒劳慰问。黄州在杭州之西，故人们常常向西眺望苏轼的方向。好友不怕留下证据，还相约结社筹钱买马，互送诗文，千里问候。此作记事，也写情谊，自然真挚。

90. On Receiving a Letter in Qi'an from a Hangzhou Friend

By Su Shi (1037－1101 Song Dynasty)

Last night the moon was bright, breezes gentle;

I dreamed I was on West Lake.

The morning came with rejoicing news:

Someone knocked with delicacies from Wu.

There were dried lichees white and round

Red snail sauce pungent and savory.

Also tea from West Monastery

Allaying sickness over the long humid river journey.

My friend is affectionate and caring

Encouraging me to travel on westward.

Sending a servant with a horse for the year

And greetings from a long thousand li away.

Let's form a poetry club

And worry not about being censored.

My heart and soul are already at the destination,

Hoping to reach River Crest Bridge by morning.

◆
◆
◆
◆

Note：Please refer to poem No. 64 for information about River Crest Bridge.

91. 杭州秋日别故友

〔唐〕长孙佐辅

相见又相别，大江秋水深。

悲欢一世事，去住两乡心。

淅沥篱下叶，凄清阶上琴。

独随孤棹去，何处更同衾。

◆
◆
◆
◆

赏：天才诗人往往能化"赋、比、兴"为无痕，如李白的"浮云游子意，落日故人情"，看似不经意的一瞥，却成千古名句。长孙佐辅的首联隐约有诗仙之风，愁见秋水和离别之情巧妙关联，从而引发读者共情。随后辅以篱下叶、阶上琴，孤帆远影衬托出一世悲欢，去住两乡的种种无奈和惆怅。可谓哀怨而不伤、繁缛而不杂，乃言可尽而理无穷的典范之作。

91. Saying Goodbye to a Friend in Hangzhou on an Autumn Day

By Zhangsun Zuofu (Tang Dynasty)

Short reunion, but we part again；

Autumn flows deep in the mighty river.

Life is full of joys and sorrows；

Between friends and destiny, one has to choose.

Leaves rustle by the fence；

A string instrument rests unplayed on the steps.

My lonely boat will carry me afar；

When will we meet again?

◆
◆
◆
◆

Note：Little is known about the poet other than the record

that he failed in the imperial exams repeatedly and led an unconventional and unrestrained life. Seventeen of his poems were passed down. This poem is one of the brightest in the starry sky of the Tang Dynasty poetry.

92. 杭州次周大夫韵

〔北宋〕蔡肇

只占西湖不占田，六莲重到欲忘年。

惭无佳句追和靖，聊取幽芳荐水仙。

对面文章能发兴，脱身朝市已称贤。

江边五月梅天雨，拟附齐舲过冷泉。

◆
◆
◆
◆

　赏：这是北宋画家蔡肇写西湖美景的诗。西湖荷花盛开之
时，重重叠叠壮观无比，往往让人沉醉流连忘返。荷花幽香，凌波
似仙，其美难以言表。西湖荷花不仅能激发人的诗兴，也能使人
忘了世俗喧嚣。五月梅雨季节，是荡舟湖上赏冷泉胜景的最佳时
节。次韵也即和诗的一种，按照原诗的韵序而作的诗。

92. Responding to Official Zhou's Poem

By Cai Zhao (? —1119 Northern Song Dynasty)

Choosing to live on West Lake, not next to rice paddies;

Among boundless lotus flowers, I forget my old age.

Abashed, my verses cannot rival those of Poet Lin;

I seek solace in narcissus's fragrance.

The lotus blooms rekindle my poetic inspirations;

Retiring from the court is a proud and sagacious decision.

In the fifth lunar moon, yellow plum rain shrouds the river;

I hope to reach Cold Spring by boat.

◆
◆
◆
◆

Note: It is a common practice for Chinese literati to

respond to other's poems. A respond could be made right on site either verbally or in written form，or it could be done at a different time without the awareness of the original poet. This is an example of the second case.

93. 送梅龙图公仪知杭州

〔北宋〕欧阳修

万室东南富且繁，羡君风力有余闲。

渔樵人乐江湖外，谈笑诗成樽俎间。

日暖梨花催美酒，天寒桂子落空山。

邮筒不绝如飞翼，莫惜新篇屡往还。

◆
◆
◆
◆

赏：梅挚是北宋勤政爱民的廉吏，字公仪，曾任龙图阁学士，故称梅龙图。《宋史·梅挚传》记载梅挚性情淳静，不矫厉，居官三十多年，清正廉明，政绩卓著，深得宋仁宗喜爱。1057年，梅龙图到杭州做官，宋仁宗与欧阳修均有赠诗。此诗先赞杭州富足繁华，再赞梅挚的性情与才华，谈笑樽俎间能成诗，与杭州之美相得益彰。最后期望好友到杭州后多多来信，诗文酬唱。

93. Sending Mei the Court Scholar Gongyi to Assume Prefectship in Hangzhou

By Ouyang Xiu（1007—1072 Northern Song Dynasty）

The populous southeast is prosperous and bustling;

I admire your confident spiritual temperament.

Enjoy your rustic life far from the political center;

Over sumptuous meals compose poems with genial ease.

Delicious wine brews during sunny pear blossom days;

When chilly, osmanthus blooms fall deep in the mountains.

I hope the courier services stop here frequently;

Do not conceal your poems, share them!

Note：This poem is related to the next. The poet bid farewell to his friend Mei Zhi，who was granted governorship of Hangzhou by Emperor Renzong.

94. 赐梅挚知杭州

〔北宋〕赵祯

地有湖山美，东南第一州。

剖符宣政化，持橐辍才流。

暂出论思列，遥分旰昃忧。

循良勤抚俗，来暮听歌讴。

◆
◆
◆
◆

赏：宋仁宗赵祯在位四十多年，仁政宽容。梅挚（994—1059）
清正廉洁，政绩卓著，在朝堂言事有体，深得仁宗喜爱、信任。
1057 年梅公仪到杭州做官，宋仁宗赐诗送行，勉励梅挚到杭州后
要继续勤政爱民，赢得百姓的爱戴。梅挚根据"地有湖山美"的诗
句，在杭州吴山修了一座有美堂，感谢上恩。《有美堂记》由文学

家欧阳修撰文、书法家蔡襄书写，并刻石于堂上。虽仅存遗址，也是文史上的一段佳话。

94. Granting Mei Zhi Governorship of Hangzhou

By Zhao Zhen (1010—1063 Northern Song Dynasty)

Known for its beautiful mountains and lake

It is the unsurpassed prefect of the southeast.

The court expects you to enlighten my subjects;

Gather your belongings, embark on your journey.

Take interlude from your scholarly life

And share my concerns and hopes at that remote place.

Be kind and diligent to the people;

I await high praise of your service.

❖
❖
❖
❖

Note: Emperor Renzong was the longest reigning emperor

of the Song Dynasty. He was considered merciful，modest，frugal and caring. Based on the first line of this poem，Mei Zhi built a hall commemorating Renzong's deep trust in his governorship. Ouyang Xiu wrote a beautiful attribute to the hall.

95. 和张按察秋山二首（其一）

〔南宋〕何梦桂

三百余年卧甲兵，天低雨露此生成。

万家都会楼台畫，千顷平湖舸舰轻。

环佩玉堂人楚楚，靓妆珠箔女盈盈。

回头万事俱尘土，惟有湖痕岁岁平。

◆
◆
◆
◆

赏：这是一首唱和诗。何梦桂生活在宋度宗时代。此时宋室岌岌可危，悲剧已成定局。诗歌开篇便指出了宋室三百多年武备废弛是历史悲剧的根本原因。第二、三联回忆南方都会杭州的繁华。遗憾的是一切美好繁华已成过眼云烟，唯有西湖之水岁岁平静安好。何梦桂的诗多有国破家亡的感怀。

95. Responding to Official Zhang's Poems about Mountains in Autumn (I)

By He Menggui (1229—1303 Southern Song Dynasty)

Armor collects dust for three hundred years;

With rain and dew, Heaven bestowed West Lake.

A city of ten thousand households, with towering mansions;

Boats float on a thousand acres of calm lake.

Lovely women adorned with pendants wander jade halls;

Charming girls blush behind pearl curtains.

Nothing is perpetual, neither nature nor people

Except the yearly ebb and flow of the lake.

◆
◆
◆
◆

Note：Like all the great historical cities around the world，Hangzhou has also seen its booms and busts. Although "dusty armor" may be the cause of one cycle of dynasty change，according to the poet，nothing is perpetual other than the ever fluctuating ripples in the lake.

96．天竺寺八月十五日夜桂子

〔唐〕皮日休

玉颗珊珊下月轮，殿前拾得露华新。

至今不会天中事，应是嫦娥掷与人。

◆
◆
◆
◆

赏：山寺月中寻桂子是杭州的一道绝美风景。每年农历八月中旬起，月满风清，杭州满城桂子飘香，历时一个多月。宋之问的"桂子月中落，天香云外飘"便是吟咏桂花的名句。这首诗写天竺寺中秋夜桂子。殿前拾得的桂花像露珠一样清新，仿佛是嫦娥从月宫里抛掷到人间的。作者用"至今不会天中事"代指嫦娥奔月、吴刚伐桂的传说。天竺寺即今天的杭州法镜寺，此诗借神话想象给佛教圣地添上了空灵曼妙的色彩，也凸显了诗人中秋赏月的喜悦心情。"珊珊"二字生动描摹了清风桂子簌簌落下的形态。

96. Osmanthus Kernels Fall in Tianzhu Temple on Lunar August 15th

By Pi Rixiu (circa 840—883 Tang Dynasty)

Jade-colored kernels drop from the moon;

Bathed in fresh dew, they are scattered in front of the hall.

Celestial happenings are beyond mortal fathoming;

Chang'e may have cast them down.

◆

◆

◆

◆

Note: The osmanthus kernels were legendary nuts descended from the moon in Tianzhu Temple on each lunar August 15th, when the moon is the brightest of the year. Only the lucky ones may find them. In Chinese mythology, the legendary Moon Goddess Change'e resides on the moon supposedly casting them to earth.

97．卜居白龟池上

〔元〕仇远

一琴一鹤小生涯，陋巷深居几岁华。

为爱西湖来卜隐，却怜东野又移家。

荒城雨滑难骑马，小市天明已卖花。

阿母抱孙闲指点，疏林尽处是栖霞。

◆
◆
◆
◆

赏：仇远为宋元易代之际的标杆人物，和白珽齐名，人称"仇白"。白龟池在西湖边，为唐代刺史李泌开凿的六口古井之一。元兵攻破杭州时，仇远刚刚三十岁，此后长期穷困潦倒，居无定所，因此"移家"在诗词中频频出现。作为赵宋遗民，西湖成了他对家园的寄托。"天际有云难载鹤，墙东无树可啼鸟"，鸟无良木可栖，鹤不能一飞冲天，唯有靠琴声浇胸中块垒，最后的慰藉也只有西湖边疏林尽处的栖霞岭，洒脱中带有淡淡的哀伤，体现了诗人排遣不去的遗民情结。

97. Residing by White Tortoise Pond

By Chou Yuan (1247—1326 Yuan Dynasty)

Accompanied by a red-crowned crane and a string instrument

I have resided in an odd alley for many years.

West Lake is a choice place in which to settle

But the east moor seems more enchanting for relocation.

The path at this wild place is slippery for my horse;

The local market at dawn already peddles flowers.

A grandma holds her grandchild points the way

Deep where trees are sparse is the hill of Qixia.

❖
❖
❖
❖

Note: As a Song loyalist, Qiu Yuan's life was unstable, as

relocation，a recurrent theme in his poems，occurred frequently. He returned repeatedly to the beautiful West Lake for spiritual comfort.

98．闻鹊喜·吴山观涛

〔南宋〕周密

天水碧，染就一江秋色。　鳌戴雪山龙起蛰，快风吹海立。

数点烟鬟青滴，一杼霞绡红湿，白鸟明边帆影直，隔江闻夜笛。

◆
◆
◆
◆

赏：词人曾为两浙运司掾属，官运亨达，喜游山玩水，多典雅浓丽的山水诗词，以《木兰花慢·西湖十景》为代表。这首词是题咏排山倒海的钱塘江大潮欲来和正来的情状。天光水色一片澄碧，染一江清秋景色；江潮涌来既像是神龟驮负的雪山，又像是蛰伏的巨龙梦中惊起，疾风掀起海水像竖起的高墙。远处几点青山像美人鬟髻，青翠欲滴。一抹红霞如同刚织就的绡纱，带着潮水迸溅的湿意。天边白鸟分明,帆樯直立,入夜后隔江传来悠扬的笛声。全词景美意美,是记游咏物佳作。

98. To the Tune of Rejoicing over the Calls of Magpie—

Viewing the Tidal Bore from Mount Wu

By Zhou Mi（circa 1232—1308 Southern Song Dynasty）

Its water is a boundless green.

Autumn dyes the riverbanks with every hue.

Suddenly, as if a giant tortoise shoulders a mountain of snow

Or a dormant dragon awakes,

Gusts upend the ocean.

A few misty mountains are lush green;

Red evening glow floats like dampened silk.

White gulls veer by taut distant sails;

A night flute melody drifts across the river.

◆
◆
◆
◆

Note: This is another tidal bore viewing poem. In the first stanza, the poet described the frightening scene of the tidal bore. The second stanza describes the calm and peaceful scene after the enormous waves have abated.

99．霜天晓角·春云粉色

〔南宋〕高观国

春云粉色。 春水和云湿。 试问西湖杨柳，东风外、几丝碧。

望极。 连翠陌。 兰桡双桨急。 欲访莫愁何处，旗亭在、画桥侧。

◆
◆
◆
◆

赏：高观国著有《竹屋痴语》一卷，其词作讲究琢句炼字，独特清新。他受到姜夔词风的影响，体制高雅，格律不侔，句法挺异。此词写西湖美景，粉色春云，西湖杨柳，翠陌望极，不同于前人荷花桂子的意象。他善于创造名句警语，词中"试问西湖杨柳，东风外、几丝碧"便是一例。"望极。连翠陌。"这种二、三字断句的体制宋词中并不多见，高观国的词多有这种格律不侔的个性表达。

99. To the Tune of a Horn on a Frosty Morning—

Pastel-Colored Spring Clouds

By Gao Guanguo (Southern Song Dynasty)

Reflections of pastel-colored spring clouds

Float on vernal water.

I ask the willows by West Lake:

After an easterly breeze

How many more green threads will dangle?

In the distance

A green embankment stretches.

My oars propel the boat faster.

Where does Lady Mochou reside?

In that pennanted tavern

By the painted bridge.

◆
◆
◆
◆

Note：Different from the Tang Dynasty poems of mostly fixed lengths，the Song Dynasty lyrics，or ci（lines of irregular lengths）were popular with literati as they could be more expressive with less restraint. This is a good example of what a skilled lyricist can do when at West Lake.

100．七绝·五云山

毛泽东

五云山上五云飞，远接群峰近拂堤。

若问杭州何处好，此中听得野莺啼。

◆
◆
◆
◆

赏：此诗作于 1955 年，毛泽东于杭州疗养之时。诗人不写西湖反写周围的群山，别出心裁又暗合诗人的豪情。五云山位于西湖南部群山之中，近与万岭山、狮峰岭、上天竺等联袂，远与南北二高峰对峙，钱塘江堤也近在山脚下。这首诗自问自答，语气流畅，喜悦流露。全诗刚健中蕴藉和婉，张弛有度。野莺啼鸣收尾也体现了作者愉悦闲适的心情。

100. Five-Cloud Mountain

By Mao Zedong(1893—1976)

Five-colored clouds drift past Five-Cloud Mountain

Circling distant peaks and brushing against embankments.

Which spot in Hangzhou is most charming?

Right here where wild orioles sing.

◆
◆
◆
◆

Note：Chairman Mao wrote many poems about Hangzhou during his numerous visits. This was written after his trip to the Five-cloud Mountain in Hangzhou.

●●● 后 记 ●●●

当我告诉几位好友我想把一些中国诗词翻译成英文时，他们不约而同地拍拍我的肩，祝我好运。 我知道，想把诗词翻译好是几乎不可能的——诗词的原意在翻译过程中不可避免地会有所丢失。 要想把这个问题说得更清楚，还需借助海德格尔。

海德格尔认为诗歌是维系人和神的媒介。 诗歌能"聆听"神/自然无声却又无所不在的述说，并通过语词的记录供人欣赏。 海德格尔还指出，我们人类也需要"敏锐的听"来抓住并领会诗人说的是什么。 自勒内·笛卡儿起，传统的"主客观"思维模式就非常盛行，海德格尔则采用了"此在"的概念，即（在场）或"在世界之中"。 他认为"存有"互为显现。 如果真是如此，那么诗词翻译就是不可能的。 毕竟，身处21世纪的我们如何能复原早已逝去的过往？ 按当代的观念，我们如何能感受、想象或体验诗人们在遥远的他乡的所做所为，而且是通过另

一种语言，裹挟着情景化的个人情感和冲动？ 海德格尔使用了
"本有/本是/成己"（分别来自孙周兴、陈嘉映及邓晓芒先生）等
本身就无法翻译的词来阐述这一纠缠不清的现象，最好的阐释
也许是"使…自在"。 简要地说，如果人类能忘却以人类中心
主义的主观视角来审视周遭万物，也许我们得以进入一个"镜像
嬉戏"的世界。 在这样一个了无偏见和前期预设的世界里，
"镜子"得以直接、忠实又真切地体现它和周遭的关系。 这里
不妨以本书第八首《诉衷情·寒食》的最后一句为例：

三千粉黛，

十二阑干，

一片云头。

诗中数字层层递减，以一种言简意赅的方式，营造出了永恒
和无常间的内在张力。 无数绝世粉黛和精美错落的楼廊早已烟
消云散，唯白云悠悠。 当下的我们也许只能在一种更宽泛的语
境中，通达诗人的脑海，从想象中窥探数个世纪前的诗人当时究

竟看到了什么，尽管这对当今的我们来说是非常的不真实。

众所周知，中国是诗的国度。犹如中古时期的英国骑士们需孜孜不懈地擦亮他们耀眼的铠甲一样，中国文人从小就勤学苦练以期留下不朽的诗作。他们无处不诗，过去几千年所留下的诗作犹如恒河沙数。唐代诗人杜甫就留下了 1500 多首诗作。杭州作为曾经的古都，相关的诗作更是举不胜举、灿若繁星。我和我的同事——四川外国语大学教授刘云春及成都大学教授刘亚玲一起耗费无数心血对浩如烟海的杭州古诗词进行了梳理，最后从公元 400 年到当代共选出 100 首诗词，其中涵盖 82 位诗人。这些诗词向世人展现了这个喧闹繁华又温暖灵动的现代都市曾经的人间烟火。

如果"诸神是神性的召唤使者"，如海德格尔在《筑·居·思》中所言，那么希望通过这些翻译，读者也能细细领略杭州美丽的风光，熟知她丰厚的历史底蕴，感受她曾经的辉煌与失落、欢爱与伤悲，以及那迷人的意象——早已颓朽的栏杆，依然飘浮的悠悠白云……——如绝世的长卷般展现！

翻译过程本身既充满乐趣又伴随苦恼困惑。为尽可能忠实于原文，我们遵循两条原则：（1）不强求押韵，哪怕只是稍稍改变诗词的原意；（2）将诗词中的每一个字视为神圣。话虽如此，有时还得寻求变通，比如中国诗人常用"断肠"一词，形容某人悲伤或焦虑到极致后的一种感受。尽管中国的读者或学者都熟知此词，我们却无法将其真的译为"小肠碎断"——这样的翻译只能影响全诗的美感。

在此我谨对以下人员表示感谢：美国新罕布什尔大学英文系教授莫妮卡·邱、伦敦国王学院的艾莉·洛克女士。莫妮卡和艾莉为诗词翻译的语词排序耗费了大量时间。本书离不开她们的贡献。此外，我还要感谢成都大学海外教育学院、中外语言合作交流中心、杭州西湖区人民政府、浙江大学出版社及杭州亚运会组委会的大力支持。作为一名杭州人，本书的翻译为本人迄今为止最具挑战性且又意义非凡的经历。

亦歌

2022 年 2 月

● ● ● Postscript ● ● ●

When I told a few good colleagues of mine that I intended to translate some ancient Chinese poems into English, they patted me sympathetically on the shoulder and wished me good luck. I know! Good poetry translation is not merely daunting—it is simply impossible! No poetry translation can be accomplished in its entirety without loss. Though somewhat true, to elucidate further, we may have to bring in Martin Heidegger.

Heidegger regards poets as those connecting earthly humans and god. They can "hear" god/nature's silent yet omnipresent voices, and then record them in words for humans to enjoy. Further, Heidegger points out that we humans on the receiving end also need "good ears" to capture and fathom what the poets are trying to say. Instead of the traditional "subject/object" view adopted since René Descartes, Heidegger calls in the notion of *Dasein* (being there) and "being in the world." He believes "beings" reveal themselves to others here and now. If so, poetry translation is impossible. After all, how can we in the 21st century try to recreate a scene wrapped in the past? How do we, in the contemporary moment, feel, think, or experience what poets did in a place remote from ours, in a different language, in their contextualized emotions and motivation? Heidegger uses the term *Ereignis* to describe this complicated phenomena, a word itself impossible to translate. The best rendition is probably "to appropriate." Simply put, if we humans can forget about our human-centered subjective view on everything around us, we may enter a kind of "mirror-play" world. It is in such a world free from prejudice and pre-disposition that "the mirror" can be direct, faithful and authentic in its relationship with its surroundings. Take the last three verses of "To the Tune of

Pouring Out Your Heart—The Cold Food Festival" as an example:

Three thousand beautiful women,

Twelve verandas,

One drifting cloud.

The poet's use of drastic reduction in numbers, verse by verse, creates an inner tension between perpetuity and impermanence through its sparse verses albeit packed with meaning. The beautiful women and inviting verandas are long gone, but drifting clouds still come and go. It is in a much broader context that we can still say that we might, just might, access what captivated the poet's mind when he created these lines many centuries ago, however inauthentic they may seem to us today.

China long has been known as a land of poets. Much like the English medieval knights who needed to care assiduously for their shining armor, Chinese literati also tried diligently from very young ages to polish their verses to perfection. They

307

created poems for every occasion. The sheer number of poems penned over several thousands of years is awesome. The Tang Dynasty poet Du Fu himself, for example, penned more than 1500 poems. Because Hangzhou is one of China's ancient capitals, poems about it are numerous and dazzling. My colleagues, Professor Yunchun Liu of Sichuan Foreign Language University, Professor Yaling Liu of Chengdu University and I spent a great deal of time perusing this ocean of poems and lyrics about Hangzhou. The 100 poems in this book range from 82 of the most famous poets from as early as 400 AD to modern China's Chairman Mao. Together, they represent this bustling modern city's warm and worldly past.

If " [t] he divinities are the beckoning messengers of the godhead, "according to Heidegger in *Building Dwelling Thinking*, we hope that through these translations, readers can savor Hangzhou's imagined scenery as much as we did and learn more about its rich history, its triumphs and losses, heroes and suitors, love and sorrows, inviting images of long-vanished verandas and still lingering drifting clouds... divine scenes indeed!

The translation process has been both enjoyable and extremely difficult. To be as faithful to the original as possible, we established two rules: (a) No forced rhyming to maintain a poem's original rhyme scheme if such an adherence changes the poem's meaning, even just slightly; (b) Regard every word in the original poems as biblical. That said, some liberties were allowed. Chinese poets, for example, use the term *duanchang*(断肠)frequently. It literary means that one is so saddened or worried by something that one's intestines break into inch-long pieces. While a native Chinese reader or scholar of Chinese poetry would understand the term, we chose not to translate it as "cracked intestines" in English, whose oddity as such would affect the overall beauty of the verse.

I wish to thank the following people for making this book possible: Monica Chiu, Professor of English at the University of New Hampshire and Ellie Locke of King's College London. Monica and Ellie spent countless hours wrangling over the poems' Enlglish words order. Their contribution is invaluable in making this book possible! I also wish to thank Overseas Educational College of Chengdu University, Center for Language Education and Cooperation, Hangzhou Xihu District People's Government, Zhejiang University Press, and lastly, the Organizing Committee of Asian Games. This has been, to date, my most challenging and rewarding experience yet!

Yige

February,2022